Praise for

SADÉ AND HER SHADOW BEASTS

'A **real ode to the power of creativity**, and the way grief can shape our worlds - both real and imaginary'
L.D. Lapinski, author of *The Strangeworlds Travel Agency*

'The middle grade book **everyone's going to be obsessed with** this summer'
Louie Stowell, author of *Loki*

'A **resonant story on childhood grief**, wrapped in vivid imagination, beautiful poetry and compelling characters'
Tomi Oyemakinde

'A book I desperately needed growing up, **a heartfelt wondrous book** that showcases the sensitivity of an imaginative British-Nigerian child'
Maria Motunrayo Adebisi

'A **fantastic, honest and uplifting** exploration of grief'
Louise Finch, author of *The Eternal Return of Clara Hart*

'With a debut like this, **I can't wait for Rachel Faturoti's next release**'
Renee Gooding

'A **fantastic take on grief** and how to deal with it'
Jamie-Lee Turner

SADÉ AND HER SHADOW BEASTS

RACHEL FATUROTI

SADÉ AND HER SHADOW BEASTS

Illustrated by Rumbidzai Savanhu

HODDER CHILDREN'S BOOKS

First published in Great Britain in 2022 by Hodder & Stoughton Limited

1 3 5 7 9 10 8 6 4 2

A CIP catalogue record for this book is available from the British Library.

ISBN 978 1 444 96357 1

Typeset in Baskerville by Palimpsest Book Production Limited, Falkirk, Stirlingshire

Printed and bound in Great Britain by
Clays Ltd, Elcograf S.p.A

The paper and board used in this book are made from wood from responsible sources.

Hodder Children's Books
An imprint of
Hachette Children's Group
Part of Hodder & Stoughton Limited
Carmelite House
50 Victoria Embankment
London EC4Y 0DZ

An Hachette UK Company
www.hachette.co.uk

www.hachettechildrens.co.uk

This is for all the kids and adults
out there who are struggling.
It's OK not to be OK.

Prologue

BEFORE: Four Months Ago

'Sadé,' Mum says, popping her head through the crack of the open door. She's wearing her favourite purple silk head scarf. 'I'm feeling a bit better now. Do you want to take a walk down to Hope Garden Centre later?'

'Yeah,' I reply eagerly, nodding. 'We can get peppermint tea there too.'

'Mmhmm, my favourite! A peppermint tea would be wonderful.' Mum's laugh is breathy. 'Your dad made me some food to eat. I'd better go downstairs.'

Once the door closes, I smile to myself because Mum is feeling better. She hasn't been feeling good for weeks.

I lie back on my bed, close my eyes, and open them to the vibrant colours of my world, which are so bright, they almost blind me. The familiar sweet and salt popcorn smell drifts over the cliff, making my stomach grumble.

Wide lavender and orange lily ombré wings block out the bright light in front of me as Nix squawks in the air, circling before landing on the grass, crowd-surfing it, and bumping into me. *It's like virtual reality in my head!*

'Hey, Nix!'

Nix's large dark-orange beak moves from side to side as she wheezily laughs in response, as if something's permanently stuck in her throat.

'You wanna play a game?' I ask, rubbing the soft velvety lilac petals on her head.

Nix nods and runs to the opposite end of the cliff, taking flight towards the vivid, endless rainbow bubble sea. Rushing to the side of the cliff, I look at the steep slide embedded into the rocks.

'You can do it,' I whisper.

I sit down at the edge, flatten my arms, lie back and slide down. My eyes water at the sudden rush of wind and I dive right into the bubble sea. Some of the bubbles on the surface are as small as a two-pence coin and others are as huge as my friend Alfie's Rottweiler, Pan. The bubbles pop around me and faint calming music plays in my ears as I float on the water and gaze up at the lilac sky.

Nix flaps her wings quickly beside me, which means she's ready to play. 'OK, Nix,' I say, laughing. 'Let's see who can burst the most bubbles.'

Her beak bursts a few bubbles before I've even had the chance to say 'ready, steady, go'. I try to catch up. As the bubbles pop, multicoloured gas drifts into the air, shapeshifting into bubble sea creatures. A large crimson seahorse swims next to our heads, a cerulean crab rises and snaps its claws, and an emerald jellyfish bobs up and down on the surface of the water. After a few seconds, the creatures burst, leaving only wisps of colour behind.

Nix squawks in excitement and lowers herself down. I hop on to her back and cling on to her soft petals as she soars upwards. She cruises just below the lilac candy floss clouds. I pull down on the edge of the clouds as we pass, stuffing sweet candy floss into my mouth, causing a sugar rush through my system. Nix dives down and speeds over my world. From the air, the maze-like Gardens stand in the shape of a giant multicoloured rose.

I pat Nix on the head. 'Down, please.'

Nix squawks and dives down, depositing me on the grass in front of three huge roses the size of footballs, where I sit cross-legged. The rapping roses. Savannah's petals are butter-yellow with white edges, Monica's swirly strawberry, and Keith's are light blue darkening to indigo near the base.

'We've got something for you,' Savannah says, dropping a beat.

Monica's petals pulse and her silky voice starts off slow. '*They can't test us, uh uh, they can't test uh, uh, they can't test us*.' Her green stem sways and her strawberry petals vibrate.

She gets faster, until all three of them are rapping together. '*They can't test us, uh uh, they can't test uh, uh, they can't test us.*' Her bud opens and closes as a low, smooth beat shakes the ground. Every time the beat drops, I'm bounced a little in the air.

While Savannah's voice is gentle, Keith's is gravelly, like he's chewing on stones. He bends his stem, and his petals vibrate. '*They say roses are sweet, they can't test us.*'

'*Stems strapped to jab, leave ya bleeding in the dust,*' Monica raps.

'Aren't roses supposed to be sweet?' I ask, laughing.

'*No colour, no size, no other flora, we're sacred, priceless just like the Torah,*' Keith raps.

Monica comes in. '*Cut, crushed or stirred, perfume, hearts or herbs, we'll keep you wondering like Dora.*'

Savannah stops the beat, turning her bud towards me. 'You can't sit here expecting rhymes, it's your time.'

Keith spreads his leaves out. 'Give Sadé some room.'

As Lion appears through the maze to hear me perform, his trembling roar ricochets through my world. I run my hands through his furry blond and brown two-tone mane.

'The others will be here soon,' he murmurs soothingly and rubs his mane against my face, which calms me.

As the animals from all over my world gather, Lion organises them, making sure the smaller animals have space to see. Kiwi, my other bird, perches by the rapping roses with his spindly fuchsia legs and pink petunia wings. Tweeting, buzzing, squealing and chirping erupts, and the butterflies flutter with their two sets of enormous transparent wings and purple trims.

'At Hope Garden Centre
when I was five,
On tiptoes I spied
the garden of Eden,
Black bamboo plants
and flowers in every season.'

The sky flashes and the candy floss clouds get even fluffier as the words fly from my mouth. The twisty vines wrap themselves around my ankles, pulling me up so I'm twirling around the Gardens like I'm on stilts. The vines sprout enormous flowers, creating a flowery platform for me.

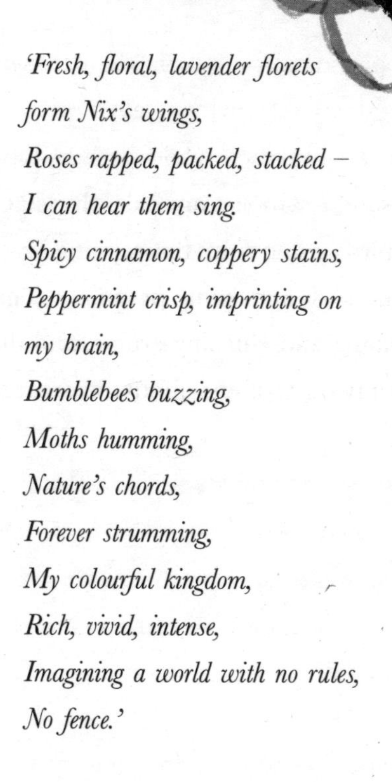

'Fresh, floral, lavender florets
form Nix's wings,
Roses rapped, packed, stacked –
I can hear them sing.
Spicy cinnamon, coppery stains,
Peppermint crisp, imprinting on
my brain,
Bumblebees buzzing,
Moths humming,
Nature's chords,
Forever strumming,
My colourful kingdom,
Rich, vivid, intense,
Imagining a world with no rules,
No fence.'

A harmonised hum pierces the air as the muttering moths swarm. Green carnation wings with spots of rusty brown, daylilies and pink hibiscus and orange irises flutter in front of me like a colourful wave. The bees wiggle their yellow dahlia and iris bulging bodies, spreading intoxicating yellow dust into the air.

Then the vines lower me back down to the ground, where Nix is waiting for me. She shakes her head and stamps her claws. I can tell exactly what she wants.

'All right, Nix, let's play another game. We can race from the Moon Gate.'

Hearing that Nix and I are racing, the animals and insects rush to meet us at the Moon Gate. I dash deeper into the forest and hop from one four-leaf-clover-shaped stepping stone to the next. They light up in green as my feet touch them. The Moon Gate is covered in fern and lavender and the plants bend forward like ballerinas to greet us.

The animals and insects part for Hen as she clucks to the front of the audience. Her soft, silky feathers are like the inside of a fluffy pillowcase and her turquoise comb stands tall like a crown. She pecks me softly on the shoulder.

'You're the fairest at judging races,' I say to Hen. 'Can you do it?'

Bending down, Hen uses her beak to draw a line in the soil where Nix and I stand. 'First one to the mushroom flowers outside the Word Tunnel wins,' she clucks. 'On your marks, get set, go!'

I dart through the forest with its tall trees. Tiger's silky white frame with the black stripes dashes through the trees as she urges me on.

'Nice speed, Sadé,' she purrs gently. 'Watch out for the nest.'

Ducking under a low branch, I swerve to avoid a nest

of bees because I know Tiger would hate it if I hurt them or myself by accident.

'Thanks, Tiger!' I shout as I speed ahead.

Nix pushes forward, her talons grazing the earth. As we pass the Moon Pool, sheets of lilac water rush down. The wind sprays some droplets in our direction.

'Ahhh!' Ice-cold water hits my face. Then I'm inside the white Word Tunnel where all the words I like from my world appear. They're always here, swirling over the walls. I run past the word 'imagination' as I leave the tunnel. Nix flies over my head and lands in front of me, right by the mushroom flowers. She won the race.

I jump on to her back and we wrestle on the ground, until we're both out of breath. Nix's forked orange tongue hangs out of her mouth, tired.

Fox comes from behind the purple weeping willow and leans against it, his reddish-orange fur clashing with the bark. 'Nix won that fair and square. Why don't you challenge *me* to a game, Sadé?'

I laugh. 'And you won't cheat like last time?'

With a paw to his chest, Fox gasps, his eyes wide. 'Me? I would *never* cheat. You know me. I swear on my two toes.'

I shake my head. 'Fox, you have *four* toes.'

'You have a good eye, Sadé,' Tiger says from in the tree as she licks her white paw. 'Don't let Fox fool you.'

'Hmm.' Fox smirks, examining a paw. 'Only four toes? Oh, you don't say,' he teases. 'You know I was only having a little fun, Sadé. How about I give you a head start?'

'All right. The first one to dive into the moon pool wins!' I shout.

Lion's deep roar sounds from the crowd behind us as Fox and I sprint through the forest.

Part One

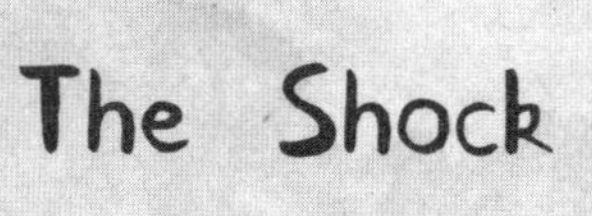

Chapter One

The sun beams through my bedroom window on Sunday morning, and it's so bright that it's hard to concentrate on *Deathless 2*. Me and Alfie are trying to rescue another village from a zombie attack. Mum never would have allowed me to play online phone games on God's day. She was the superglue of the family, and now everything's unsticking, changing and falling apart. My thumbs fidget across the cracked phone screen as I watch Alfie's player fling a quicksand paintball at one of the zombies, causing it to sink into the ground. *Yes! 30 points.*

Teni's snores sound from the bed on her side of our room. Her side looks completely different to mine; mine has white walls, funny animal prints and strings of fairy lights shaped like the moon and stars over my bed. Teni's side is painted dark grey, with a matching bedspread and black furniture. She calls it minimalist.

Teni's snoring is honestly as loud as the number 36

bus's blaring horn. My sister sneaked in late again yesterday after everyone was asleep.

As I throw a firework paintball to distract another zombie, Grandma's singing sounds from outside. It's as high-pitched as the birds from my world when they're talking to each other.

'Ara ẹ di de ẹ bami jó eniyan mi, ẹ ba mi yọ fun oluwa mi to gbe mi ga.'

My people stand up and dance with me, rejoice with me, for God has lifted me up.

Grandma knocks and peeks her head through the crack in the open door. 'Kaaro, omo mi. Lo mura fun ile ijọsin.'

Good morning, dear. Go get ready for church.

'Morning, Grandma.'

OnceUponaTime: going to church we can play later
Alfiedagreatest: k

Shutting the bedroom door behind me, I take a deep breath as I walk past Mum's purple study door, which is next to my room. It's where her words live.

Tolani's room, which she shares with Grandma, is open, but Dad's door is closed, meaning he's downstairs.

The smell of Dad's strong, steaming coffee burns my

nose hairs as I reach the bottom of the wooden steps leading into the large living room, which Mum painted purple to match her study. To the right, Dad's sitting at the round kitchen table with the matching soft teal chairs. He flicks his *Sunday Times* newspaper out, so it covers almost the entire surface and then he licks his finger to turn the page. Using his free hand, he stirs the rich, smooth ogi in the bowl in front of him. There is a plate piled with freshly fried akara beside it.

Dad hasn't cooked in months, so this is surprising. I've missed Old Dad's cooking and the rest of Old Dad too – New Dad's a sleeping ghost. I know he's not *really* a ghost because his car is parked outside, his shoes are by the door and the fridge magnet says, 'Dad is home'. He *is* home, but not really.

Mum used to make Dad soft like the inside of a Creme Egg at Easter. Sometimes, Dad would complain about Mum leaving her spa stuff around the house. But one time, my sisters, Teni and Tolani, and Mum and me came back from eating at our favourite Chinese restaurant – the one with the extra sticky ribs that glued my fingers together.

When we came through the door, we saw Dad on the sofa wearing a bright-green face mask, his feet in a bath of salt, and his fingernails so polished that they were gleaming. Mum's eyes creased like fresh folded laundry as she laughed, warm tears trickling down her face, as she removed the cucumbers from his eyelids and kissed each one.

But that was before; these days Dad's hard now. Like a Creme Egg, but without the creamy middle.

As I sit down, Dad slides the ogi and akara towards me.

Is Old Dad back or is it a trick?

'You're not going to make me eat by myself, are you?' he asks. 'I added something extra to the akara this time. You're going to *love* it.'

I fiddle with the spoon for a second, staring at him, before pouring the creamy condensed milk into my ogi and mixing. 'Thanks, Dad.'

I scoop a spoonful of ogi into my mouth and bite into the akara. I tap my chin as Dad watches me, an expectant look on his face.

'Garlic?' I ask, after a few more chews.

Dad lifts his hand and high-fives me. 'You got it. That's my girl.'

Stirring the thick ogi, my mind drifts to school. The thought of going back soon makes my stomach crumple in, like the lilac scrunchie holding my hair in place.

Old Dad was the best listener ever. If there was an award for listening, he would've won it. Gazing into the ogi as if it holds all the answers in the world, I whisper.

'Dad?'

He looks up at me and stops chewing.

'I don't know . . . school starts tomorrow. I don't know if . . . I'm ready . . .'

Dad grips on to his spoon so tightly that I'm scared it's going to bend. Clearing his throat, he gets up from the table without meeting my eyes.

I knew Old Dad wasn't back.

The silence is broken when Teni and Tolani come downstairs, with Grandma following slowly behind. Teni's long, black knotless braids are packed into a high ponytail. The ends fall down her back as she walks through the arch between the living room and the kitchen. Grandma looks at my burgundy jumper dress and nods in approval. I prefer printed T-shirts and jeans to dresses. Grandma's wearing an orange ankara dress, which matches Nix's wings in my world, and a white head tie.

Tolani tucks back hair that's escaped from my bun before touching her cropped afro to make sure it still looks good. *It does!* She has a mohawk with four twists on each side.

Tolani takes a banana from the fruit bowl in the centre of the table, peels it and bites into it, watching Dad move into the kitchen to empty his food into the bin and wash his bowl. 'Dad, are you coming with us?' she asks, raising her voice so he can hear her.

If anyone was going to make Dad come to church, it would be his favourite, my oldest sister Tolani, aka Tolly, but he's as allergic to church now as Alfie is to not getting into trouble.

'Of course he's coming with us,' Grandma replies.

Coming out of the kitchen, Dad clears his throat. 'I'm not going.'

Grandma grips the back of my chair. 'Ṣe iwọ yóò lọ titi lailai ni? Iyẹn a ba ọkàn Enitan jẹ.'

Will you stay away for ever? That will hurt Enitan's heart.

'Don't mention my wife's name!' Dad shouts. 'And there is nothing for me in church.'

Only New Dad shouts at Grandma and ignores me.

Tolani lowers her voice. 'Dad, it's all right, you don't have to come with us – it's just that we're going to visit Mum's grave after. It's her three-month anniversary.'

'What are you going there for?' Dad splutters. 'Enitan isn't there.'

Tolani flinches and Grandma sighs.

Dad's eyes flicker to me, remembering that I'm still sitting here. 'All of you can go, but Sadé is not allowed to go to that place. She's far too young for that.' Heat flushes through my body.

Far too young. My family always use that as an excuse for everything.

I'm not allowed to visit Mum's grave, but I still get to see her in my world whenever I like. Mum's always there now. Dad's footsteps leave the kitchen.

'Je ka lo,' Grandma says, and we leave for church.

My best friend Funmi nudges me and points at Auntie Gladys's wig sliding off her head at the front row of the children's church. A small smile breaks out on my face. Funmi can *always* make me smile, even when I don't feel like it.

'That wig is gonna get up and walk,' Funmi giggles.

'Hello . . . hello. Can everyone sit down?' Uncle Dan stammers from the front.

We take a seat. I'm in between Theresa and Funmi. Theresa is my other church friend. Funmi swipes through dance videos on her phone, leaning towards me so I can look too. 'I can't wait to go back to school,' Funmi whispers excitedly. 'The talent show assembly is next week and then it's nearly time for auditions.'

At least someone is excited about school starting.

Funmi scrolls back and forth between videos. 'I dunno what dance the twins and me should do. What about this one, or this one?'

Vanessa and Antonia or 'the twins', as we call them, are in the same year as us, but in a different tutor group. The twins live on the same street as Funmi, and they all dance together most weekends.

Funmi is sparking with energy about the talent show like an AA battery. I already know their dance will be the best.

'I like the first one,' I reply.

She nods. 'Yeah, me too – their leg work is so on point.' Funmi finally looks up from her phone. 'Are you going to audition?'

I wish I could audition. I would perform, and my words could fly like my muttering moths, but I don't write any more, and it doesn't matter anyway because I'm not like Mum. She was a firefly, lighting up a *whole* room with her words.

'Nah, I don't think so.'

'Can everyone quieten down, please?' Uncle Dan tries again, shifting from one foot to another.

A younger girl screams behind me as a boy tries to push her off her chair and she pushes him back. He tumbles to the floor with a loud thump, waking Auntie Gladys up.

Auntie Gladys scratches her head and adjusts her wig,

looking around to check nobody saw it slipping. 'Uncle Dan, have you started yet?'

While Joshua with the gap between his two front teeth picks his nose and flicks it, Theresa gets up and brushes at some gum stuck on her skirt. Uncle Dan hangs his head and shuffles out because no one *ever* listens to him.

Auntie Gladys's bones crack as she stretches her small body. She is wrapped in a grey woollen cardigan. 'Since you don't want to behave for Uncle Dan, I'll be teaching you today instead.'

Auntie Gladys flips open her dusty bible. 'We're going to learn about Noah today.'

'I miss your mum and her stories. When Auntie Gladys teaches us, it always makes me fall asleep,' Funmi whispers to me.

'Yeah, your mum made everything fun,' Theresa adds from my left.

They're right – Auntie Gladys's voice is about as interesting as the salad bar in Pizza Hut. If Mum was here today, she'd make us imagine that we were inside Noah's boat, and she'd get in an imaginary rowing boat beside us to bring the story to life. I wish I could be more confident like Mum.

I wish Mum was still here to write with me.

Chapter Two

Monday

'Ow!' I shout as a scrunched-up piece of paper hits the side of my head.

'Sorry, Sadé,' Alfie snickers. 'It was for Callum but his head's so small, I missed it.'

Mr Sanders's laser eyes drill into me – as if he thinks I'm having way too much fun in his maths class.

Alfie's overgrown blond hair flops to the side as he dodges Callum's deadly kicks under the table. Alfie is messing about *again* but that won't stop him from getting top marks on the quiz. Last term Dad asked, 'Do your friends have two heads? Why are they getting top marks and you're not?' Alfie must have two heads – or two brains at least.

Our finished maths quizzes form mini mountains in front of Mr Sanders as he marks them. His thin, pale wrist flicks upwards and sometimes downwards at his desk. Occasionally he smiles; more often he sighs at the marks.

A sudden whiff of sweet and salt popcorn floats in from

my world, but it smells burnt. The whiteboard at the front of the room flickers; for a brief second, it is a purple weeping willow. One of my butterflies flies through the door. When I blink, everything is back to normal. *Did I imagine that?*

Mr Sanders says my name and places my test in front of me. He pronounces it 'Say-dee' and I say 'Shaa-day', but to my dad it's 'Fọláṣadé' with a tight 'e' at the end like a Nigerian drum skin.

I look down at the marked test in front of me. The score is hidden, but I know it's bad from all the red-marker crosses next to my answers and Mr Sanders's face, which is like stone, hard and unmoving. A deep sigh spreads from the top of my head down to my toes, until I'm choking in his disappointment. Turning it over, I see the big red 30% at the top of the page.

I hear a low, warning growl coming from somewhere in the classroom.

Mr Sanders sent a letter home last year, before everything changed for good. I watched my parents open

it from the gap in the bannister.

'Didn't you hear what her maths teacher said at parents' evening? Her grades are a cause for concern.' Mum fiddled with her purple headscarf.

'Please don't stress too much,' Dad had replied. 'You need to get some rest. Why don't you lie down, and I'll make you something to eat?'

Mum shook her head. 'I can't keep anything down – it'll just go to waste. We need to talk to Sadé. Why didn't she tell us she was struggling?'

That was one of the last times Mum was Mum – before the hospital swallowed her up and turned her into an octopus with tubes everywhere. My heart beats fast to the sound of the beeping hospital machine in my head.

Was it my fault?

'Watcha get, Sadé?' Alfie asks, pulling me back into the room.

He flashes his 98%. If Funmi was here, she would be showing me a similar mark, but she's at the dentist to check her braces. I half-shrug. Below the desk, my stomach is bubbling, and my hands are sweaty.

'I got eighty per cent,' I lie.

Alfie cheers like he's watching his football team at Stamford Bridge. 'She shoots; she scoresssss!'

Mr Sanders's eyes burn into Alfie. Callum cheers too,

while Alfie pumps his fists in the air and claps. Sometimes I think Alfie does this stuff on purpose.

'Carefree, wherever you may be. We are the famous CFC!'

Everyone starts laughing around us. I laugh too, pushing the low maths score far back in my mind.

'That's it, Alfie Miller. Get out of my classroom, *now*!' Mr Sanders thunders. 'If you're not careful, you'll end up expelled like your brother.'

Alfie shrugs. 'Ryan is solid.'

When Ryan was at school, he held the record for the most detentions ever! But Alfie isn't scary like Ryan, who hangs around the shops near the estate with his friends drinking alcohol – or Ògógóró as Dad calls it. It makes them walk wonky and fumble over words.

I scratch out the number on the page like those thoughts in my head. If my grades don't get better by half-term, I'll get a bad report. My pen curves as I write the number six.

Six weeks until the end of term. If I do well in maths, I can get a good report and then they'll all see. They won't need to be concerned about me. Everything will be all right.

Chapter Three

I usually love English lessons. I've loved words ever since Mum first took me to Hope Garden Centre for story time. On the way there, I would pat Oscar's head. Oscar is the friendliest Labrador who is *always* sitting outside the local newsagents, guarding it.

I would tell Mum all about my world and we'd share poetry and stories and write them in my journal.

Words and plants in symmetry. Words get me. They shake, shout, dance, prance, and my words – my poetry – powers this amazing world that's imaginary and only I can see.

But now my journal is as empty as the bottle of ketchup in our fridge.

I'm sitting with Funmi in English class. Trina's eyes flicker to us and she whispers something to Jas, my ex best friend, behind her clear nail polish and they cackle like evil witches. Funmi, Alfie, Jas and me all used to be friends in primary school.

'Are they whispering about us?' Funmi asks me, tucking a piece of hair behind her ear.

'Yeah,' I reply.

Holding up a worksheet Mrs Karoma floats back to the front of the classroom.

'Year Eights. We will be doing a few lessons on descriptive writing before we move on to Shakespeare, and do you know what that means?' Her eyes sparkle like Jas's glittery headband, even though I know Jas hates glitter. 'It means lessons full of exciting words we'll be sharing with each other.'

How can I share when my word well has dried up? Leaving only scattered letters, weighing down my tongue.

'I've given everyone an image. Now, I want you to look at that image and use your imagination. Write down all the things you can see, hear, touch, taste and smell. I'll give you ten minutes.'

My image is of a shark and fish swimming underwater. I try to think about what Mum would write, but my mind is empty. I can't do it, so I squeeze my eyes tightly together and lean over the image, falling into my world.

* * *

My stomach feels bottomless as the tall, tickling green stems of the crowd-surfing grass catch me, as usual, and flip me on to my back.

'Ouch!'

I jump off the grass because it's spiky, but the grass wasn't prickly before. *What's going on?* The same burnt sweet and salt popcorn smell from maths class clogs my nose. It *was* coming from my world.

I shiver. It's both too hot and slightly cold in here – the temperature is broken. Usually, the warmth toasts my body like a hot water bottle. Colour bleeds like ink over the tropical forest, the bubble sea with no more bubbles, over the Sanctuary, the Gardens and into every small crack, but the colours have faded, like when you wash your favourite jeans too much. Standing up on my tiptoes, I bounce and raise my hand to grab some candy floss as the sky bends towards me.

Instead of being fluffy, the lilac candy floss is sandy and slips through my fingers. I try to pick more. This time it's sticky. Shaking my hand, the lilac slime hits the grass, burning a small hole into the ground.

What's wrong with my world?

A familiar laugh comes from behind me, sounding like chiming bells.

I turn. Mum's full, springy black afro is tied in her favourite purple headwrap, the one with the big bow at the front, and her gold studs gleam in the light.

'My Sadé,' she says. 'I hope you packed all your books for school. You know what I always say to my students: *you can't forget if it's already done.*'

I reply, 'Yes, Mum. I packed it last night.'

She smiles sweetly at me, her eyes crinkling at the corners. 'Good girl.'

A large muttering moth the size of my hand settles on my shoulder, chirping away in his language. He flutters his wide poppy-flower wings; they're spotted with black dahlias, and yellow daisies brighten up the edges. Mum vanishes.

'Spinggy deeeep!' the moth cries in its own language, but I understand it.

'You've seen something running in the forest?' I gasp. 'Nix, where are you?'

There's a loud squawk before Nix lands on the edge of the cliff. As I run my fingers through the soft lavender petals on her head, she makes a cooing sound.

'You ready to fly?'

Nix spins around excitedly and I duck, right before her long tail hits me. Nix dives off the cliff. I dive off the cliff too and land on Nix's back. As she races through the air, the ride is bumpy and the cold wind rushes into my eyes.

The trees are hazy as she weaves in and out of them.

On the ground, Kiwi flaps his petunia wings and his tall legs chase after a black blur. Lifting my body off Nix's back, I try to get a closer look at whatever it is.

'Go closer, Nix.'

She dips into the forest, right above the creature. It's not a blur any more. From behind, the creature is tall and lean, with reddish-orange patches in its black, matted fur. Its hind legs dart forward.

'It's getting away!' I shout. 'Vines!'

The vines burst through the ground from either side. They join in the middle to trip the creature up. As the creature leaps over the trap, another vine bursts out of the ground, tangling itself around its leg and pulling the creature against a weeping willow.

I pat Nix's head. 'Put me down.'

We land and I climb off Nix. Taking small steps towards the creature, my heart pounds against my chest. The creature tilts his head up and starts laughing. It is Fox, but he doesn't look or sound the same. He is no longer on all fours but stands on his hind legs. Fox's long, black claws grip his dark, furry stomach as he bends over. The laughter stops and I notice that his once green eyes are now glowing orange.

Fox's eyes track my movements. 'Ah, Sadé. There you are.'

'Fox? You look . . . different,' I croak.

Fox bares his grey needle-like teeth at me and frothy saliva forms on his bottom lip, dripping down on to his matted fur. 'You're the reason why your world is different and why I've changed.'

Please don't stress too much. You need to get some rest.

'I – I did it. My grades . . . It *was* my fault.' I was right before. 'I knew it. I hurt Mum.'

My world is like this because of what I did to Mum. As my chest tightens, I try to breathe, but I can't. There's not enough air. The pounding sound of my heart is all I can hear.

She's a cause for concern.

I stagger and tiny dark spots appear before my eyes. Bending down, my body trembles and my insides feel numb.

Why didn't Sadé tell us?

'It's all my fault,' I rasp.

Fox bites into the vines and he disappears into thin air. Someone touches my shoulder and I'm pulled out of my world.

* * *

'Sadé?'

Mrs Karoma is crouching beside my desk with her eyebrows squished together. Everyone is looking at me. I feel myself getting hot.

'Sadé. I've been calling you for a while. Are you OK?' she asks kindly, lowering her voice. 'You're shaking.'

Wiping the tears from the corner of my eyes, I nod my head.

Mrs Karoma looks at me for a long moment, before whispering so only I can hear her. 'You're needed at the counsellor's office. They sent Ms Davis down with a note. Will you be OK going with her?'

Ms Davis, one of the teaching assistants, with sandy-brown hair and round eyes waits for me at the front of the classroom.

As I walk towards the front of the class, Funmi's eyes burn small caterpillar holes into the side of my head. My Kickers feel like weights on my feet. *What did I do wrong now?*

Callum is always calling the counsellor's office the 'Mad Office'. *Does coming here make me mad then?* But then Callum did recently mix five solutions together in science class and we had to stand outside in the cold for *twenty minutes* so we wouldn't inhale poisonous gases. I'm taking what he says with a pinch of seasoning.

I stare up at the 'Mindfulness & Wellbeing' poster on the pinboard outside the office. Freddy from my form says the Black girl on the poster and me are twins because her skin's the colour of espresso, deep and brown as Dad likes it, and we have matching hairstyles with cornrows braided up into a bun, and button noses. Next to that poster is one for the talent show. The same poster has been put up *all* over the school, counting down to the auditions and the talent show. The talent show assembly is tomorrow. If I can't even get good grades to keep Mum here, I definitely can't audition in a few weeks.

Shifting my bum on the hard plastic chair, I replay what Fox said in my world over and over in my head, until my thoughts are as tangled as my afro before wash day.

The old wooden door creaks open and a young white woman with rainbow hair and a big fringe appears. The silver patch in her fringe matches her eyes. She smiles widely at me, like that big grin emoji.

'Hey there!' the woman with rainbow hair exclaims. 'I'm Ellie. Come on in, Sadé.'

Ellie shuts the door behind us and ushers me to a seat before sitting down at her desk. Her head just reaches over the mountain of papers perched on it. 'It's *great* to meet you. I'm the new counsellor for Hope Wood Secondary.'

I don't say anything. Ellie must be broken because she's just sitting still, staring and smiling broadly – like the big teeth emoji now. *You think turning her off and on again will work?*

Eventually she starts talking again. 'Don't worry,' she reassures me. 'I won't keep you for too long. I wanted to tell you about an *exciting* app we're trialling here at Hope Wood Secondary called "Support You and Me". It's a grief support app.'

The words spiral and curl over each other like strands of spaghetti. Ellie's voice is a boomerang thrown far away, but the words head back towards me, hitting the side of my head.

'. . . students who have been affected by grief meet anonymously for weekly group chats with counsellors like me. The app operates like WhatsApp. The main difference is that the sessions will be held on the app during school time and the chat is moderated by me.'

It sounds as fun as the WhatsApp group I share with millions of my cousins from Nigeria I've never even met, which is no fun at all.

Ellie continues. 'It's for young people like you who are grieving. I know this is a difficult and sensitive topic. Is it OK with you if I continue?'

A flash of heat rushes through me, boiling my blood.

'Sadé?' Ellie speaks. 'Would you like me to stop?'

As I rub my forehead, a whiff of sweet and salt popcorn from my world floats by my nose, but when I sniff again, the smell's gone. 'No.'

'Oh good. You seemed lost in thought for a second there.' Ellie leans forward. 'What are your thoughts?'

I shrug. 'I don't know.' But I *do* know.

'That's fine. Can I tell you some more about the group chat?'

I nod.

'OK, great. I facilitate the group and my aim is that the app provides a safe and supportive space for you to explore your feelings around the death of your mother. The group has three other students that meet once a week.'

Three other people who'll know what I did.

'Will they know it's me?'

'No, they won't. We meet online, anonymously, to

discuss thoughts and feelings around grief. It can be comforting to hear others' experiences which might be similar to yours. What are you thinking?'

'So, it's . . . like messaging?'

'Yes, exactly that, but you won't know who you're messaging. You'll each have unique usernames, which you can choose – of course. The sessions are during Tuesday lunchtimes, for six weeks . . .'

'Six weeks!' I blurt out.

Ellie waves her hand in the air as if she's swatting an annoying fly away. 'It is important for you to know that your dad signed you up for it because he knows what an opportunity it is to meet other students like you. How do you feel about that? Did you know?'

I thought the school was making me do it. My dad can't have signed me up because he says therapists poke their noses into other people's business, but I don't want to tell Ellie that, so I stay quiet.

Ellie pulls out a crinkly sheet from the leaning tower of papers. 'I have some details here as I appreciate this is a lot to think about. Take a look and let me know what you think. It includes instructions on how to download the app. I hope you feel able to join.'

I pick up my rucksack, which is still covered in animal pins I collected from Hope Garden Centre. Before I started secondary school, badges were cool. Funmi says they're not cool any more, but I don't really mind.

Ellie taps the side of her head. 'Oh, and if you consent and are OK to go ahead with the group, there are one-to-one session each Friday, to give you an opportunity to chat with me about anything that comes up for you from the chat.'

A message pops up on my screen.

New Message from Tolani

Don't be angry at me.
I signed you up for a support group. I know Dad's been acting weird and I think talking to someone about Mum will help.

I *knew* it. I knew Dad would never sign me up. Swiping the message away, I stuff the phone back in the bottom of my bag. My oldest sister Tolani always does stuff like this, but Teni would never.

'Are you all right, Sadé?' Ellie asks. 'Is this uncomfortable for you?'

Talking to Ellie won't help. I can't get a bad report and that's what happens to students who don't do well. Nobody can get hurt again because of me.

Clutching my bag to my chest, I reply, 'I've

got science now.'

But I don't have science because it's breaktime.

Ellie looks at the clock on the wall with a frown, but she says, 'If you're sure you're OK, then you can go. I hope to see you on Tuesday!'

I wish I could go to one of my secret spots around school and hide out, but instead I take the longest way to our bench, dodging the bigger upper-schoolers in their black blazers, red striped ties and crimson jumpers. My navy lower-school jumper and blue-striped tie stick out like a sore thumb.

Amina, Teni's friend, spots me in the corridor as she fixes the pin in her black hijab. 'Hey, Sadé,' she sings, using her free hand to wave.

My 'hi' comes out as a small squeak, even though it sounded louder in my head.

She smiles brightly. 'You're so cute.'

Other upper-schoolers say hi too and let me squeeze past them in the packed hall. They only know me because of my sister Teni. *Everyone* knows Teni. She's popular.

When I reach our bench, I see Funmi with her shoulder-length, pressed black hair hiding her face like a curtain as she bends over her phone. Looking up, she stops texting and starts asking questions.

'What happened? Did you get in trouble?' Funmi's eyes go wide, making her look younger.

I want to tell Funmi about the app, but I remember yesterday, when New Dad didn't want to hear what I had to say. *Sometimes it's easier keeping stuff inside.* My words keep coming out wrong anyway.

'Erm, nothing happened. I forgot to sign in.' Then I have an idea. 'Have you decided on the dance for the talent show auditions yet?'

I knew it would distract her. Funmi jumps up from the bench and smooths down her black pleated skirt. 'Yeah. Why don't I show you now?'

Chapter Four

As I twist my key in the door, the smell of frying onions drifts through the gap. I imagine them sizzling in the pot. The spices catch my throat, making me cough. I'm going to miss Grandma's cooking. She's been here since Mum's funeral, but she's going back to Nigeria soon.

'Sadé! Ṣé ìwọ ni?' Grandma asks.

'Yes, Grandma, it's me,' I answer, entering the kitchen, which is as bright as the rest of the house, with its bubble-gum pink, aqua and yellow cabinets.

The golden-brown skin on Grandma's face wrinkles as she smiles at me like I'm the last cheesy Dorito in the bag.

I see bundles of spinach stacked on the white surface by the sink and a chair beside it. I quietly groan because I know what's coming. I hate cutting spinach! There's always lots of it and every time I think I've cut loads into the bowl, it cooks down to like *one* leaf.

'Can you help me cut the spinach?' Grandma asks.

I pick up the knife and start chopping. Grandma's bum looks like a broken clock hand moving backwards and forwards as she sings next to the steaming pot. *Mum's favourite song.* Grandma glitches and suddenly Mum's dancing in front of me in her luminous-orange floral dress. Head tilted back, Mum used to twirl me around the kitchen, until we were both dizzy and laughing. I squeeze my eyes shut because Mum can't really be here. A stinging pain, followed by heat, rushes to the tip of my finger.

'Ow!'

The knife clatters to the floor.

'Be careful, Sadé.' Taking my finger, Grandma runs it under the freezing-cold tap water, and when it stops bleeding, she wraps my finger tight with a plaster and it reminds me of pigs in blankets from roast dinners. Grandma kisses my finger with a loud smooching sound, making me laugh.

'Ṣe o dara bayi?' she asks.

I nod. 'Yes, it's better now.'

Grandma takes over cutting the spinach and I play with the plaster on my finger.

'Ki lo wa l'okan re?'

What is in your heart?

My mouth opens, and the secrets of the day come gushing out, like the water from the tap. Apart from the bad grades. I don't want Grandma to get hurt from worrying about me too.

'. . . I know Dad will be angry when he finds out about the support group, Grandma.'

Grandma looks like she's thinking deeply, as she lets water from the tap flow into the bowl of cut spinach, washing out all the dirt and grit.

'Why don't you try this support group out? Inu ikoko dudu ni eko funfun ti n jade.'

White corn paste comes out of the black pot.

'Mum used to say that to me too.'

'And who do you think taught her,' Grandma replies, puffing out her chest. 'Do you remember what it means?'

'I shouldn't judge a book by its cover.'

She nods. 'Bẹẹni. Just wait and see, Sadé. Life can surprise you sometimes. And don't worry about your dad. We all just need to give him some time and you know he works many hours at the hospital.'

Soon the sweet smell of efo riro fills up the flat and me, Grandma, Teni, Tolani and Dad are packed around the table. Soft pounded yam swallows fill the long silences. Then, with his plate wiped clean because Dad never wastes anything, he pushes his chair back and goes to the kitchen to rinse his plate.

Teni's phone vibrates on the table and Tolly watches

her. Teni picks it up. Tolly frowns. Teni is addicted to her phone.

'O ṣeun fun ounjẹ maami,' Dad says to Grandma. *Thank you for the food, Mum.*

The stairs creak under Dad's weight as he walks back upstairs to his dark cave. Mum always had the curtain open in their room, but Dad keeps it closed. Teni's plate rattles in the sink as she dumps it in and jumps on to the mustard sofa in front of the TV.

I wash my plate and go upstairs. I stare at my journal on the white bedside table. I wish I could release all the words that have been trapped inside me, pouring them out of my head on to the page.

A game invite pops up from Alfie, but I can't think about playing now, so I decline.

Alfiedagreatest: ☹

Closing my eyes, I fall back on to the bed and enter my world. The one place where my words work. The one place that was once perfect.

* * *

Opening my eyes, I sit up on the cliff.

'Mum,' I say, looking around. 'Mum! Where are you?'

My voice rebounds through my washed-out world, which is strangely quiet.

I need to talk to her about school and about Ellie, the woman with the rainbow hair.

It was *never* quiet here before. The birds aren't chirping, there is no buzzing or squealing and the animals aren't gathering to hear me. Looming over my world, I look down at my bubble sea and there are no more colourful bubble animals or soft music.

A muttering moth hovers in the air by me, its furry orange antennae tickling my ear. 'Zowzy pasghetti?' he asks.

Throwing my hands up in the air, I reply. 'Of course I wanna know what's happening. I promise I won't get upset.'

Taking out a large, curved leaf, he reads out a tally. 'Wiggly piggly. Ittily. Spindingy.'

The lilac sky flashes deep purple, setting a dark glow over my world.

'Are you sure that the insects have been injured?' I ask. 'How many?'

The moth flutters one wing. 'Spingy. Dupdee.'

'Ten! Insects have *never* been injured here before.'

The moth flies off after delivering its message.

Nix carries me deep into the forest and drops me outside the Gardens. I need to talk to the rapping roses.

There's a rustling behind me. I turn to see a set of scrawny marigold claws.

I gasp.

It's Hen. Her feathers used to be white and fuzzy, but now they're fluorescent green and scanty with marigold edges. Hen would strut around, showing off her silky feathers, clucking for everyone to hear. Now she is quiet and hangs her head. Nix wails beside me.

'Hen, what's wrong with you?' I ask.

'Everything here is wrong. It used to be safe,' she clucks weakly. 'Fox has already gone. Tiger and Lion have gone too. I'll see you soon.'

'Gone where? Where did they go?' I shake my head. *Where will Hen see me if not in this world?* 'But – but I can fix this. I'll get good grades and then everything will go back to the way it was before.'

Hen disappears.

Trekking through the forest, I weave through the Gardens' maze and slump down in front of my rapping roses.

Savannah's pale bud opens. 'What's got you down, Sadé?'

'Yeah, tell us about that frown,' Keith says.

Monica agrees in her smooth voice. 'Mmm hmm.'

Sighing, I murmur. 'It's this world. It's all changed because of what I did. Even your petals . . . they're off.'

I breathe in, hold the air and let out a thin train of purple smoke. The words stir up inside me and I try to get them out.

'Why don't you let it out, Sadé?' Savannah asks.

'The strings are tight and digging in.

Stirring.

I am stirring inside . . .'

I struggle to find the right words and slump back down in front of the rapping roses. Their petals are withering before my eyes. It's all wrong.

* * *

'What's wrong?' Tolani asks, and my eyes pop open. 'And who are you talking to? You know what they say about people who talk to themselves . . .'

After one year of Psychology at her London uni, Tolani thinks she knows *everything* about everything. Sitting up, I pick at the loose thread hanging off my duvet cover. The mattress dips lower as Tolani joins me on the bed and moves close to me.

'Sadé, listen. I'm sorry I didn't tell you about signing you up for the support group.'

I stop picking at the thread and look up. 'Why'd you do it? Does Teni know too?'

'No, I haven't told her.' Tolani puts her hand gently on my shoulder. 'I saw a leaflet on the board by reception when I came to pick you up last term. Counselling can really help, you know. I've been talking to someone. You used to write poems in that journal of yours every day, but you've stopped. Counselling might help you write again.'

Tears gather behind my eyes and I stand up. 'I don't need help.'

'Sadé, where are you going?' Tolani asks. 'I'm trying to talk to you.'

I'm a dragon spewing fire. Rushing out the room, I shut

the bathroom door and drop down on to the closed toilet seat.

I think about asking Ellie to leave me out of the support group, but she'd ask why. What would I say? That it's not Dad who signed me up, but Tolani? *Would she think badly of Dad?* I don't want to get Tolani in trouble either because at least she sticks up for me, especially when Dad is as hot and cold as my world feels right now.

Tolly knocks on the door. 'I'm sorry. You know that I just wanted to help you.'

After a few seconds, I wipe my eyes and slowly open the yellow door. When Tolani sees my face, she pulls me into a tight hug, and I rest my head against her warm jumper.

Tuesday

Grief Support Group Chat [1]

Ellie[moderator]: Hi! Welcome to Session 1 of the support group chat. It looks like everyone has signed in so we can get started. My name is Ellie, as you know, and I'll be your counsellor. We're going to keep this chat short today as an introduction.

The purpose of this group is not to have all the answers or give advice, but to give you a safe space to talk about your experiences and provide you with some suggestions on how to cope with your feelings in the future.

Grief is a personal process which takes some time to come to terms with. We will all experience it differently.

Today, we will be getting to know each other and establishing the group agreements. I'm so excited for you all to be here.

Anon05: i don't want to be here

I nod as the reply pops up on my screen. Adults always think they can force us to do stuff.

You'reDaObiWan4me: lol
Ellie[moderator]: Thank you for the introduction @Anon05! You can start off our icebreaker. Can you tell us two truths and one lie about yourself?
Anon05: sure!!!! i don't want to be here i don't want to be in this [message has been redacted]
Ellie[moderator]: Language which may cause offence will not be tolerated in this chat. Please consider alternative ways to express yourself. @Anon05 I would suggest taking a moment to reflect on your frustrations before rejoining the group.

OK. Let's continue.

You'reDaObiWan4me: lols
BendItLikeC: I can write with both hands

I've never left london

when I was 3 my brother slide-tackled me when we were playing football and I broke my leg in 2 places

You'reDaObiWan4me: the first one is a lie obvi
only 1% of the population is ambidextrous 🤗
BendItLikeC: Trex what?????
You'reDaObiWan4me: 😆
ambidextrous – people who can write with both hands
BendItLikeC: what about you?
You'reDaObiWan4me: star wars the best thing ever created, I want to be a comedian, I can rap
BendItLikeC: stars wars has the cool lightsaber fights
You'reDaObiWan4me: star wars is more than just lightsaber battles.
that's like saying marcus rashford is only a footballer
BendItLikeC: ???? marcus helped with free school meals
and that book club thing
You'reDaObiWan4me: see
Ellie[moderator]: Which one do we think is @You'reDaObiWan4me's lie?
BendItLikeC: the comedian one
You'reDaObiWan4me: incorrect

I'm very funny

Ellie[moderator]: What about you @OnceUponaTime?

Me? I don't know what to write and the words aren't coming. I don't want them to think I'm rude like Anon05.

~~I'm good at~~

~~I used to write poetry~~

~~I can see a world outside this one~~

OnceUponaTime: favourite colour is purple. I can ride a bike and I like English

BendItLikeC: everyone can ride a bike. I learned when I was 3

Dad tried to teach me, but I couldn't find the brakes and went flying over the bars into a big bush of stinging nettles – that was the last time I tried!

You'reDaObiWan4me: that one's the lie. The bike one

am I right @OnceUponaTime?

I'm never wrong

BendItLikeC: 😒

OnceUponaTime: yeah

Ellie[moderator]: Great, now all the introductions are done. I would like to start off explaining the word 'confidentiality'. What does it mean?

You'reDaObiWan4me: it's like when princess leia trusted r2-d2

BendItLikeC: is he that robot thing

You'reDaObiWan4me: come on man. r2-d2 is more than a robot. He had the galaxies in his hands.

Ellie[moderator]: Yes @You'reDaObiWan4me. You're right! It is similar to that. Confidentiality essentially means that whatever is said in the group stays in the group.

We're going to come up with the rules of the group together. The first one can be confidentiality. In order for us not to breach confidentiality, I want to ask everyone in this group to anonymise their names and details of stories when sharing. Any other ideas?

You'reDaObiWan4me: be on time

I'll provide the entertainment

Ellie[moderator]: Thanks @You'reDaObiWan4me be on time is the second rule.

Ellie[moderator]: anything to add, @BendItLikeC @OnceUponaTime @Anon05?
BendItLikeC: we can say what we want
Ellie[moderator]: Excellent! Yes. That's another rule. Feel free to be open in this group. Think of this as your safe space. But you must always remember to respect others, which is the final rule. Respect.

Time's sprinting fast and I haven't said much, and the chat is almost done.

Ellie[moderator]: If you don't feel like commenting in a session, that is fine. I will be asking from time to time for everyone to give me a thumbs up to make sure you're listening, even though you might not be commenting. Let's try it out now. Is everyone with me?
You'reDaObiWan4me: 👍
BendItLikeC: 👍
OnceUponaTime: 👍
Anon05: 👍
Ellie[moderator]: Wonderful! Thanks group. @You'reDaObiWan4me can you share the rules with the rest of the group?

You'reDaObiWan4me: confidentiality, be on time, say what we want, respect

Ellie[moderator]: Thank you! I'll be checking in with each of you soon. Before we finish the chat, there is a box behind reception for this support group – only reception staff know who can have access. It will be our communication box for anything you might want to share with the group. I have left a journal in there for each of you. Reception staff do not know what it is for and why you are collecting it. You can bring it to each session and write down any thoughts or ideas. Does anyone have any questions?

Chapter Five

Chris, the school receptionist, heaves a plastic box stuffed with journals on to the counter and places it down by the talent show audition sign-up sheet.

I dig through the box. Without seeing my name, I know mine's the deep-purple one with animal outlines on the front in white. When I open it, a note from Ellie lodged in the spine falls out.

Dear Sadé,

Writing is freedom! This is yours to do with as you wish. Spread your wings.

Ellie

Sitting on a chair in reception, I take out a pen from my bag and rest the new journal on my legs in their black school trousers to write:

This notebook belongs to Sadé. It's mine to mark muddled words mixed with rhymes hovering over the black lines. The words are locked in a parallel prison. Break them out, set them free so they swing high, growing like trees, touching the edges of the sky and the dark bottom of my bubble sea. These words won't pop. They won't disappear into thin air but cling on like koalas.

Clapping echoes down the corridor. I forgot that the talent show assembly is happening right now in the main hall. I walk towards the noise to peek through the window. I see rows of students watching Mr Lawrence, the drama teacher, talking. He is waving his hands in the air.

The door creaks as I pull it open and everyone stares at me like I have twenty toes growing out of my forehead, including Mr Lawrence. I dip my head down and shuffle in.

Mr Lawrence sighs, rolling his eyes. 'Another latecomer. Come in and find a seat,' he says. 'I won't be repeating myself so keep up.'

Spotting Funmi and the twins, I quickly sit down beside them.

'Where did you go at lunch?' Funmi asks. 'I was looking everywhere for you.'

‘I went to the library . . . to do homework.’

Funmi’s face pinches as if she’s sucked a sour lemon. ‘Why didn’t you tell me? I would’ve come with you.’

Mr Lawrence leaps across the stage like a frog, drawing our attention back to the front. Usually, Funmi and me do everything together because her brother is always busy. If Alfie’s brother won the most awards for being bad at school, Funmi’s brother, Femi, wins them for being good. He’s good at everything.

‘One of the last talent show winners has even gone on to star in a McDonald’s advert,’ Mr Lawrence says. ‘Isn’t that ah-mazing?’

‘Dressed up as a hotdog with no mustard,’ Alfie whispers, his face appearing between us.

‘Alfie. What are you doing here?’ I ask. ‘I thought you had football practice.’

‘I’ve had it,’ he replies, holding up his muddy football bag.

Funmi shuffles away from the smelly bag and almost falls off her chair.

Alfie chuckles. ‘I came to watch.’

An older girl with long honey-blonde hair pulled up into a ponytail pinches Alfie. ‘Stop lying.’ She’s wearing a crimson jumper over the school’s football team shirt.

'Ow, man. Charlie, that hurt,' Alfie moans, rubbing his arm.

'Serves you right,' Charlie replies. 'He only came for the free sweets at the end.'

Mr Lawrence claps, getting our attention. His eyebrows furrow in disapproval. 'The talent show will be slightly different this year. We will still have our three winners, chosen by the judges, but there will be a new crowd favourite vote too. How ah-mazing is that?'

Alfie mimics him. 'Totally ah-mazing.'

I giggle, but it *is* amazing. Imagine winning something like that. I've spent hours watching real spoken-word poets. When they speak, everyone listens but when I do, nothing goes my way.

'I'll be sending around details about the auditions and talent show to all form tutors. Now . . .' Mr Lawrence shimmies his shoulders. 'Let's shake things up a bit! As usual, we're going to see if any of you kids would like to come up here and give us a pre-audition taster!'

Hands shoot up as high as my crowd-surfing grass, but I keep mine trapped under my armpits.

Don't pick me. Don't pick me.

Mr Lawrence's voice is muffled, deep in a tunnel. 'Hmmm. Let's see . . .'

'Nessa, put your hand up higher,' Funmi says. 'I've got

our dance shorts in my bag!'

This was a big mistake. I shouldn't be here. I shrink lower, hoping it'll make me disappear as Mr Lawrence's finger scans the hall. 'You, you and . . .'

He's going to pick me. I know it. My stomach is a bottomless pit as excited whispers spread through the hall.

I can't go up there.

It's all wrong.

I'll embarrass myself. I'm nothing like Mum. She was the real performer, not me.

Funmi's mouth moves but no sound comes out. I bend down as a swarm of butterflies from my world circle me. Their papery wings move in slow motion and change from purple to gold. *What's going on?*

I try to get up but the butterflies crawl down the back of my school shirt, while vines burst from the ground, twisting around my ankles, pinning my feet down. The world feels like it's shaking or maybe it's just my body. I curl up like a beetle and shut everyone out.

'Sadé, what's wrong?' Funmi asks.

'Out of my way!' Mr Lawrence's voice sounds like he's at the bottom of a swimming pool.

His face appears before mine, but he's all blurry. 'Just listen to my voice,' he says, speaking slowly and clearly. 'You're going to be fine. I think you're having a panic attack. Just listen to my voice.'

One of the other teachers claps their hands and begins leading people outside. 'Come on, you lot. Let's move this outside.'

Everyone forgets about me and leaves through the double doors. Only Alfie and Funmi stay, standing either side of Mr Lawrence as he talks.

'Don't worry about the others. You're safe. Just listen to my voice. Try and breathe.'

His voice seeps through my mind like oil, removing the rust, and air rushes into my lungs.

'Is she going to be OK?' Funmi asks worriedly. 'Sadé's mum died before the summer holidays.'

'Ah, of course, thanks for reminding me, Funmi.' Mr

Lawrence leans in. 'Everything is going to be OK, Sadé. That's it. Just like that.'

The last of the fog evaporates from my brain, but now I feel like I've run a marathon.

'Why don't we go and find Nurse Coleen?' says Mr Lawrence. But I quickly shake my head.

'In that case, I recommend some fresh air,' Mr Lawrence says, with a small smile on his face.

'Yeah, my football coach says that outdoor stuff is the best,' Alfie chips in.

'If you don't feel better, go and see Nurse Coleen right away,' Mr Lawrence advises.

I stumble from the chair. My friends help me outside and the crisp air blows against my face.

As we reach the playground, one of my muttering moths appears in front of me.

'What are you doing here?' I ask.

Bending down, his antennae tickle my ear. 'Spindingy breepee.'

'What do you want me to see?'

He takes off, weaving through the crowd and I trail after him. 'Excuse me . . . sorry . . . Excuse me.'

'Breepee supeee.'

The moth extends his antennae and points towards a small puddle of purple goo by a crack in the school building. I look up – goo runs from the top all the way down to the bottom of the building. The crowd swells. Someone shoves me in the back trying to get closer to the crack, and then my crowd-surfing grass appears out of nowhere, rebounding me back.

The moth disappears as someone grips my elbow.

Funmi leans in close to me. Her face has the same look she had at Mum's funeral.

'Sadé, stay with me and Alfie.' She links my arm. 'Are you feeling better now?' she asks. 'Do you think Mr Lawrence was right – were you were having a panic attack?'

Hiding my trembling hands in my blazer pocket, I copy and paste a smile on to my face. 'I just . . . I wasn't feeling well, but I'm fine now.'

'I wanna take a picture of the crack,' Alfie interrupts. 'Do you think a zombie is gonna jump out, Sadé?' He leans forward, trying to take a clear picture.

Mrs Williams moves through the small crowd. It's hard to miss her red hair, cut into a sharp bob.

Her voice is a whip. 'Alfie Miller! You know you're not allowed your phone out. Put it away. There's nothing to see here. Just some bad cement.'

Mrs Williams is our headteacher, or the ice queen as

Alfie likes to call her because she's frosty and one blink from her could mean a week's detention.

There's rustling and a growl behind me in the bushes but, when I turn back, there's nothing there. Alfie said he saw the fattest rat the size of a cat running round school once. I pray it's not that!

'Oh my days, look who's coming,' Funmi says.

Jasmine, Trina and Freddy walk in our direction, then stop in a huddle near us. I don't know what's worse – the beast in the bushes or the three of them.

'I watched your new video, Trina,' Jas says.

Ever since Trina turned thirteen, she started her own YouTube channel and has been posting make-up tutorials, but I don't think they're that good and she can't even wear it to school. All I know is that Teni's winged eyeliner is the best – I don't know how she does it!

Trina flips her waist-length hair that is light-brown at the top and fades to blonde at the bottom. '*So* many people have watched the video. Like two thousand people already.' Trina's voice is like an old hoover, loud and annoying.

'One day her nose is gonna fall off from all the lying,' Funmi whispers.

I cough and Trina's eyes snap to mine.

'What are you looking at?' she asks, moving her neck from side to side.

'Nothing,' I whisper.

'What did you say?' Freddy asks, snarling at me. He is a scary volcano, ready to erupt at any minute.

Alfie appears beside me. 'Clear off, Freddy.'

'You're just jealous,' Trina smirks, crossing her arms. 'No one would watch something with a dummy like you in it.'

My throat dries up. 'I'm . . . I'm not dumb.'

'*I . . . I . . .* Speak properly then. You were too scared to get up in the hall. Is there something wrong with you, Saydee?'

'Her name is Sadé,' Funmi says.

Holding Funmi's arm tighter, I mutter, 'Leave it. I don't want you to get in trouble.'

Funmi steps past me. 'Why don't you just leave her alone, Trina?'

'Oooooooh!' A crowd forms around us.

Freddy shoves Alfie. Alfie stumbles before jumping into Freddy's face and pushing him back.

'Fight! Fight! Fight!'

Trina swings her bag at Funmi but Funmi ducks, pulling on Trina's black blazer to stop her and I hold on to Funmi. Jas just stands there.

'Get out of my way!' Mrs Williams's voice bursts through the crowd. 'What is going on here? All of you! My office. Now!'

It's only been a week, and this is the second time I'm sitting on an uncomfortable plastic chair outside an office. Instead of Ellie with the rainbow hair, I'm waiting for Mrs Williams and she's much worse. While this is Alfie's second home, I've never been inside her office. Eventually, Mrs Williams opens her door and the six of us march in. It's cold inside, just like her.

Mrs Williams lowers her towering body on to her throne and we stand in a line in front of her, waiting for her orders. She signs a few letters on her table, pretending we're not here. After what feels like for ever, Mrs Williams puts her pen down and clasps her hands together, leaning forward. 'So, who wants to start off by telling me what exactly happened?'

The others all start to talk at the same time.

'Stop!' Mrs Williams shouts, holding up a hand. 'One at a time.'

Alfie, Funmi and I tell the truth, but Trina and Freddy lie. Their lies about us starting the fight are taller than the shelves in the room and the stacks of paper on Ellie's desk the other day.

As Mrs Williams's eyes roam over us, I try hard not to fidget. Alfie says she can smell fear.

Mrs Williams sighs and leans back in her chair. 'I've heard enough. I'll be calling your parents to notify them of the incident today. You're dismissed.'

It's not fair. They started it! My stomach somersaults because I know New Dad's going to be mad. After the letter home last term, I promised that I'd do better at school. *And I need to do better to stop anything else bad happening.*

Freddy shoves Alfie as he walks out. I hold Alfie back by his bag straps before he ends up in another fight. Once the other three have gone, I let his straps go.

'Funmi, I'm sorry about ruining the assembly for you,' I say. My arms hang loosely by my side. 'I – I know you were *really* excited about it.'

Funmi links arms with me. 'I was, but it's all right.' She shrugs. 'It was just the assembly anyways. I can't wait for the *real* auditions.'

Chapter Six

'Sadé,' Dad calls as soon as the front door slams behind me. 'Come in here now, please.'

I shuffle into the living room, where Dad is sitting in his blue hospital scrubs. Grandma is next to him in an old red bubu. Dad's legs are crossed and vibrating as he bounces his knee up and down. I knew he was going to be mad.

'Did I send you to school to be fighting?' Dad asks, his voice getting louder with each word.

I shake my head and look down at the hardwood floors. If Mum was here, she would've calmed Dad down.

Grandma reaches out to Dad. 'Michael. Kilode ti o duro tẹtisi nko te mi n so? Omo yii o kin ja.'

Why don't you wait and listen? Your daughter doesn't fight.

She nods at me with a smile.

The words rush out. 'They were picking on me, but it wasn't my fault.'

'It's not your fault? What about this one?' he asks,

throwing down an envelope on to the glass table in front of the sofa. 'Why didn't you tell me you were still struggling?'

Would Old Dad have listened if I'd told him?

Picking up the envelope, I see it has the school stamp. I bet it's about maths. *Why can't I do anything right?*

She's a cause for concern.

Why didn't Sadé tell us?

'What's going on?' Tolani asks, coming down the stairs in a black tank top and jeans.

She plucks the envelope from my hands and removes the letter. She scans it, then scans me, before looking at Dad. 'Dad. The school have suggested extra maths sessions for support. You shouldn't be shouting at Sadé. Mu—'

Dad picks up his glasses case and storms off. He never wants to talk about anything any more.

My eyes sting.

I turn towards the staircase, but Tolani's hand stops me. 'Sadé, wait.'

'Jẹ k'o lọ,' Grandma says. 'She needs to be on her own.'

Tolly drops her hand and I run upstairs into my room and dive on to my bed, probably wrinkling my school uniform.

The purple journal that Ellie gave me peeks out of

my bag. Reaching over, I tug it out and find a fresh page to write:

I'm scared.
Scared and forgotten
like a rotten piece of
gum glued under the desk.
Failing.
This is a maths test
I'm failing because
I can't run for ever,
I'm at the edge of the cliff
and need air more than ever.
The emptiness wraps around me
like Thor's red cape,
but I'm not an Avenger.
They're stronger.
I can't escape.

Grandma knocks gently and comes into the room. I close my journal, hiding it under my pillow, and pull the covers right under my chin. She sighs and nudges me so she can get under the covers too. We lie there side by side.

'I'll talk to him for you,' she says. 'Please, don't worry.

He's just angry with everything right now.'

She's always telling me not to worry about New Dad, but I am.

Grandma holds my hand. 'I know you would never get into a fight. Is someone bullying you?' she asks.

I shrug.

'Is it something to do with the friend you fell out with . . .' Grandma clicks her fingers as she tries to remember. 'Josephine.'

'Jasmine, Grandma,' I mumble. 'And yes, she was there.'

'Did I ever tell you the story about how your mum stopped her bullies?' Grandma asks.

My head tilts back. 'Mum had bullies?'

Grandma laughs. 'Yes, omo mi.'

Yes, my child.

'She only told me about it *years* later, but I remember that day. When your mum was schooling, I cooked and sold akara. Your mum was always complaining when it was time to help me. But one day she got up early and said she wanted to make her own akara for school. I didn't know at the time that these two children had been stealing her lunch . . .'

'What did she do?' I ask, clinging on to her words.

'She got a handful of ata rodo and blended it well in that akara and took it to school.'

Ata rodo is a hot pepper and it feels like your tongue

is burning if you put too much in when you're cooking.

'Those children stole her food that day. After they ate that akara, they rushed to the lavatory because their bums were on fire.' She makes the running motion with her hands and tips her head back to laugh. 'They *never* bothered your mum ever again.'

I smile widely. 'I can't believe Mum did that.'

My mum was patient, always. Even when Funmi and I were playing in the house and we broke her new vase with the fresh sunflowers Dad bought her.

'Your mum had that fire deep inside. O le ma ni anfani lati rii, Fọláṣadé, ṣugbọn ina kanna ni o wa ninu rẹ.'

You might not be able to see it, Fọláṣadé, but you have the same fire within you.

'I really don't want you to go, Grandma,' I say, snuggling deeper into her soft body. Grandma says nothing but squeezes me tighter. *What am I going to do when Grandma leaves? Why do all my favourite people leave?*

Once Grandma goes to bed, a game notification pops up from Alfie.

Alfiedagreatest: u all right?
OnceUponaTime: sometimes it's a lot with everything
Alfiedagreatest: stuff with ur mum?
OnceUponaTime: yeah
Alfiedagreatest: ☹
let's hunt some zombies
u can take it all out on them
it's better than keeping it in
OnceUponaTime: thanks Alfie
let's hunt zombies

Chapter Seven

Friday

Back on the plastic chairs outside Ellie's office, I'm trying to scrub out everything that happened yesterday with a rubber in my mind, but the faint lines still show. My phone pings with a notification from the *Deathless 2* app. Opening it up, I click on the quivering gift box at the bottom of my screen.

Alfiedagreatest has gifted you Storm Techs (purple edition)

Yes! I've always wanted these Storm Tech boots because they have loads of cool settings. When we're fighting the zombies, I'll be able to levitate and blast towards them with the rocket setting. This must've cost Alfie most of his points. Alfie is the best. I guess he's trying to cheer me up.

OnceUponaTime: I love the boots thanks Alfie

'Sadé, are you coming in?' Ellie asks, holding her door open.

Ellie's hair is now a bubble-gum-pink colour. I drag my feet inside her office, and she closes the wooden door behind me.

'So, Sadé. What's the what?'

I don't want to talk about what's happening. Ellie is like a zombie from *Deathless 2* who keeps coming back – but I can't get rid of her by throwing a paintball.

'Nothing.'

'Nothing?' She winks at me. 'Something must be happening. Perhaps it's hard to think of what to say and it's easier to say nothing.'

It's a huge, ginormous something. I'm failing at school, my world is weird, and New Dad's been as cold as the last ice lolly at the bottom of the freezer.

Ellie slaps her leg, and I notice a small wings tattoo on her ankle as her flared velvet trousers rise. 'OK. So, I just wanted to check in with you after the first support group session. How did you find it?'

'It was OK.'

'Hmm,' Ellie replies. 'I noticed you were pretty quiet.

I am wondering if it's because it might have felt scary. Or perhaps you wanted to be quiet and observe. Oh, before I forget, did you collect your notebook?'

I smile. 'Yeah. How'd you know I'd like that one?'

She points down. 'Your bag. Writing in a new journal is like putting on a fresh pair of socks and wiggling your toes around to get comfortable. Journaling is also a great way for you to process your feelings at your own pace and make an emotional connection with difficult experiences, such as the death of a loved one.'

'What about if someone doesn't wanna make a connection?' I ask.

'Hmm. Think about a TV and its power source. How do you make sure the TV will turn on to watch your favourite show?'

'Ermm. I make sure it's plugged in?'

'That's correct. So, this –' she holds up her right hand – 'is a person and their grief, thoughts, and everything, and then this –' she holds up her left hand – 'is the difficult experience. So, for example, a loved one dying. It's important to bring the two together, like a sandwich, and find ways to deal with these emotions. One way is through a support group or journaling or talking to people like me, or you might find a way that works for you. But it's important not to avoid experiencing these intense thoughts or feelings because it can affect our mental health and our ability to enjoy life. Are you finding it hard to make the connection?'

'No,' I blurt out. 'I mean . . . I'm fine.'

Except for the fact that my bad grades hurt Mum and now my world isn't safe.

Ellie just watches me, which causes me to squirm in my seat. 'It can feel uncomfortable to make that connection. How are you doing in school?'

The letter from school flashes in my head, along with Dad's shaking leg.

'Sadé?'

Does she already know how bad I'm doing? I bet she does. I bet *everyone* knows.

'Yeah,' I mumble. 'Maths is hard sometimes . . . but everything's fine.'

Ellie nods and picks up a white unicorn mug to take a sip. 'I'm sure you have it handled, but if you were struggling and needed support, are you aware of where to go to?'

I almost groan because the letter from school mentioned it. 'Yes, the Learning Lab.'

'Have you considered going?' she asks.

I flip the idea around like a pancake in my head before I answer. If I do better at maths, then my report will be good and my world can go back to the way it was before. My grades caused all of this, after all.

'I can try.'

'Trying is good enough.' Ellie grins.

Chapter Eight

Later that day

Alfie and I are deep in a game of *Deathless 2* on our bench as upper- and lower-schoolers rush past us.

'Come onnnnn! I totally hit the zombie,' Alfie grumbles, running his fingers through his freshly-cut blond hair.

'Hold on,' I say, leaping over an abandoned car with a bag full of paintballs in the game. 'Copy me.'

I challenge a zombie to a dance-off. Once it's distracted, I hit it with a firework paintball. An explosion of colours lights up the screen.

Callum says 'girls don't game', but my *Deathless 2* score is higher than his, so I think he's just jealous. Tolani said he was being prejudiced and his thinking was twisted. She's right about that part because one time Callum swore he could do the splits during PE, but he ended up twisted like plaited bread and they had to call an ambulance.

Sticking his tongue out, Alfie copies me, and we wipe out all the zombies. 'Yes! Next level.' He lowers his phone and pumps his fist. 'You feeling better today?'

I think about what Ellie said about journaling and the support group helping me to make an emotional connection. 'Not really . . . not yet.'

'I don't even know why you guys play that game any more,' Funmi interrupts, and we grab our bags to head to English.

Once someone says something isn't cool, Funmi will stop using, watching or doing it. Things were easier when we didn't care what other people thought. That's another reason why I like the animal badges on my bag. It reminds me of those before times.

'My mum almost cancelled my dance classes because of Mrs Williams calling home,' Funmi complains. 'She kept on saying that Femi never got in trouble. I'm lucky. I said I was sticking up for you.'

I hate that my friends are getting into trouble because of me.

'How come your phone didn't get taken?' I ask Alfie.

He flashes me a cheeky grin, like he's just bitten into the most chocolatey cake ever. 'Pan got into the cupboards again and covered the house in baby oil and crisps. Mum lost it and forgot to take my phone away.'

When Alfie used to tell me stories about home, I thought he was making it all up, but Alfie has really seen *everything*. He has five siblings and he's the middle child. Alfie's used to people crying over an empty cereal box, dogs swimming in milk and water fights in the middle of the night. I never know how he gets anything done in his house, but he *still* does better in maths than me.

As we're walking through the corridor to English, Teni's head bobs up and down in front of us, with her braids piled on top of her head in the usual bun for school. Teni's crowd of friends surround her, including Ashaunna. *Everyone* knows Ashaunna. She's Head Girl, sings lead in the school choir, she's a sports captain *and* she's a poet. I wonder if she's auditioning for the talent show too. Unlike me, I bet she wouldn't struggle to find the words.

Teni sees me. Moving me away from the crowd, with her arm around my shoulder, Teni says, 'Tolly told me what happened with Dad and the letter. Is he not talking to you?'

'Not really,' I reply softly. 'It's kinda the same as before.'

Bending down to my level, Teni looks me straight in the eyes. 'I'll talk to him. Don't worry about it. You know what he's like.'

Grandma told me not to worry about New Dad and now Teni too. New Dad is smothering Old Dad, squeezing the good out of him.

Teni stands up tall and catches up with Ashaunna, who is waiting for her by the lockers. 'See you later, Shadz,' she calls over her shoulder.

Once we're inside English, Mrs Karoma calls for our attention at the front and points to the board. 'Year Eights. I'm setting you your first assessed piece of creative writing for the year. It'll be on the subject of bullying for Anti-Bullying Week. Freddy suggested it. Thank you, Freddy.'

Freddy has a smug expression on his face and leans back casually in his chair. I wonder if he's trying to be good after Mrs Williams called home last week.

Mrs Karoma smiles. 'And . . . I will choose a few to be displayed at reception.'

I can write my homework in the new journal Ellie gave me. She'd said that writing in a new journal is like putting on a fresh pair of socks and wiggling your toes around to get comfortable.

As Mrs Karoma loops through the classroom, she clicks her fingers together. 'And I want you to have fun with it. It can be a poem, a song, a short story, an essay or even a rap. Any piece of creative writing that could go up on the wall.'

'*They can't test us, uh uh, they can't test us,*' I whisper, while doodling in my English book.

'Yes, Sadé.' Mrs Karoma nods her head. '*They can't test us, uh uh, they can't test us.*'

Alfie drums on his table with two pencils, shooting me a grin as he tries to hold the beat.

'Can you rap?' Mrs Karoma asks me.

I want to say that I love words, but I sink lower in the chair.

Trina snickers, whispering to Jas before giving me a dirty look. *What did I ever do to them?*

'Well, I'm impressed. That sounded like a rap to me,' Mrs Karoma says, walking back to the front of the class. 'Please hand in your homework before our next lesson. Now, in today's lesson we're going to be writing letters where you describe one of your most memorable days . . .'

As soon as I get home, I dive on to the sofa. It's like I'm in a museum because my house is never this quiet, so I switch on the flatscreen TV for background noise. All I can think about is Trina, her laughter creating a mini storm at the bottom of my stomach.

Dad shuffles into the living room wearing his blue hospital scrubs and sinks into his favourite reclining chair with a deep sigh, scratching his low-cut hair. He shuts his eyes.

'Hi, Dad.'

Peeling open his eyes, Dad's gaze focuses on me, tucked in the corner of the sofa. 'Oh, hi, Sadé.'

Old Dad would've asked me about my day, but New Dad only seems to have enough energy to say two words.

I can't believe it. Our favourite black-and-white film

comes on the TV. Black-and-white films used to be my and Dad's thing. The couple on screen are swing-dancing, and the man spins and flips the woman he's dancing with over his shoulder. With a steaming fresh bowl of sweet and salt popcorn between us, Old Dad would sing along to all the songs, even though his voice was terrible. It would make me laugh so hard I'd cry.

Dad's eyes flicker to the screen. Grunting, he lifts his body out of the chair and leaves the room.

Journaling is a great way for you to make an emotional connection.

I smooth out a fresh page in the journal.

* * *

Closing my eyes, a cold breeze trickles down my spine and I'm on the cliff. It's quiet. Too quiet. No sounds fill the air. It's the first time I've ever felt truly alone in my world. If Tiger was here, I know she'd help me understand. She'd help me get everything back to normal, but she's gone.

The dense plant fist opens for me to climb into, and I tower over my washed-out world like a streetlight. I think about Trina and Jas. My pen moves across the page and then I say the words out loud.

'Bullies destroy, uproot,
Their vines choking lives
so we can't shoot,
Character is built like a tree,
Their words chop down first.
Wait.
They say words can't hurt me,
cut me,
bruise me or
kill me.
The words wriggle down
deep, seeping,
worming and squirming in my brain.'

At first, nothing happens, and nothing stirs, but then my washed-out world flickers and a small spark of lilac colour reaches the outer corners, like a watercolour painting.

* * *

I open my eyes and tear out the page from my journal, to hand in to Mrs Karoma for my homework.

Tuesday

Grief Support Group Chat [2]

Ellie[moderator]: Hello! I hope everyone has their brand spanking new journals out, ready for the session. I can see everyone is here. Let's recap the rules of this group. Can anyone tell me them?

You'reDaObiWan4me: confidentiality

be on time

say what we want

respect

Ellie[moderator]: Perfect, thanks @You'reDaObiWan4me. In last week's session we got to know each other a little and I hope to continue that this week. We're also going to be talking about understanding grief and loss.

Everyone's journey with grief is different and this group is not meant to fix everything or tell you how to grieve. If you ever feel uncomfortable with a task or a question, you can pass, but it would be great if you could contribute. I'm going to pair you up and I want you to interview your partner.

A little icon should pop up with some questions and your job is to tell the rest of the group about your partner. You can use the private messaging feature. Here are the pairings:

@OnceUponaTime @Anon05

@You'reDaObiWan4me @BendItLikeC

I groan. The librarian's eyebrows dip low, and he points to the 'No talking' sign. I don't want to be paired with Anon05.

Ellie[moderator]: You have five minutes to find out as much as possible. Go!

PRIVATE CHAT

OnceUponaTime is typing . . .

Anon05: are you writing an essay? just ask me a question

I knew Anon05 was going to be rude.

OnceUponaTime: what's your favourite colour?
Anon05: don't have one
OnceUponaTime: everyone has a fave colour
Anon05: nah
OnceUponaTime: how many brothers and sisters do you have?
Anon05: 0

He doesn't have any! I know Tolani can treat me like a baby sometimes, but I can't imagine not having my sisters.

OnceUponaTime: I've got 2 sisters
Anon05: fave lesson
OnceUponaTime: English. Yours?
Anon05: i hate school but french isn't that bad

My eyebrows rise in surprise. French? Ms Dubois is super strict, and her lips never twitch during her lessons.

Anon05: i wanna go to France one day
OnceUponaTime: my dad makes croissants from scratch
Anon05: that's sick
i like crepes best

OnceUponaTime: with strawberries
Anon05: yes
and chocolate sauce

After a few minutes, I realise that talking to Anon05 is all right and we actually have some things in common. We carry on like this for a while and find out even more about each other!

OnceUponaTime: what do you wanna be when you grow up?
Anon05: i wanna grow up that's it

GROUP CHAT

Ellie[moderator]: Time. OK @Anon05 @OnceUponaTime can you tell me something about your partner that we didn't know?
Anon05: @OnceUponaTime likes english
has 2 sisters
OnceUponaTime: @Anon05 likes French
wants to go to France
loves spaghetti hoops
Ellie[moderator]: Great! The other group.
You'reDaObiWan4me: @BendItLikeC wants to be a footballer, doesn't like peas

BendItLikeC: @You'reDaObiWan4me can make his eyes vibrate LOOL

You'reDaObiWan4me: it's true

I can hum and whistle at the same time too

Anon05: weirdo

Ellie[moderator]: @Anon05 I want you to consider the impact of that word.

Anon05: sorry

Ellie[moderator]: Thank you. I hope this task has allowed you to learn something new about someone else in the group. Great work so far!

We're going to move on to our first activity in understanding your grief. It's called 'fact or fiction'.

If you agree with the statement you post 'fact'. If you don't, you post 'fiction'. I may ask you to expand on some of the statements.

Ellie[moderator]: Here's the first one.

People die in different ways.

You'reDaObiWan4me: fact

BendItLikeC: Fact

OnceUponaTime: Fact

Anon05: fact

Ellie[moderator]: OK. Let's expand on that. What are some of the ways people die?

You'reDaObiWan4me: death by gran's slipper

cancer

BendItLikeC: car accident

Ellie[moderator]: My thoughts or feelings can make someone die.

Anon05: Fiction cos mrs williams would be six feet under

she has it in for me

Anon05 and Alfie would get on.

Ellie[moderator]: @Anon05 once again, please consider the impact of your words.

Anon05: sorry

Everyone else says fiction.

Ellie[moderator]: It's my fault that my loved one died

Fact.

BendItLikeC: Fact

Ellie[moderator]: @BendItLikeC why do you think that?

BendItLikeC: cos it's true

my best mate Tim died cos of me. he went in the sea by himself cos he was waiting for me. I was late. he was always going on about it

Ellie[moderator]: It must be hard feeling like you are responsible but it's perfectly normal to feel this way because death can remind us how little power we have over it. Death can happen to everyone and anyone, but **@BendItLikeC**, remember: you were not in charge of the sea. Why don't you try to replace those kinds of thoughts with more proactive ones? For example, 'I am not in charge of the sea. I had no control over what happened.'

BendItLikeC: I'll try it

Ellie[moderator]: Great! Thank you @BendItLikeC – I think you'll be pleasantly surprised!

Let's move on to the next one.

It is best to stay in control and keep a stiff upper lip

I think Dad has a stiff upper lip because it's hard and doesn't move, kinda like him now.

Anon05: fact
OnceUponaTime: fact
Ellie[moderator]: It's OK to let our emotions out. It's healthy and part of the process.
And the last one. A funeral service, or a memorial service is a good way to say goodbye to our loved ones who died.
OnceUponaTime: fiction
Ellie[moderator]: Do you want to expand @OnceUponaTime?

I didn't say goodbye to Mum the way I wanted. On that day, the rain didn't rain, and the sun didn't sun. That day was the worst of the worst before it was even done. It was a grey and black day; no oranges or purples and my brain was going around in circles.

OnceUponaTime: I didn't get to read out one of my mum's stories at the funeral like I wanted

Mum hated anything 'normal'. She thought it was boring. Mum loved colour and wanted everything to be a celebration. Mum didn't

want anyone wearing black and she wanted the day to be full of happy words. Dad didn't listen.

Anon05: because we're the kids and they're adults
it's not fair

It's really not fair. Everyone, including Dad, thinks they can make decisions for me.

OnceUponaTime: sometimes I feel like my dad doesn't listen to me
like what I say doesn't matter
Anon05: parents are always like that
my dad was
they always wanna say something but can't take it when u talk back
Ellie[moderator]: What all of you have to say matters. Especially now and that's why we're here. Don't let anyone make you think that what you say doesn't matter.
@OnceUponaTime why don't you find a time to do something in memory of your mum?
Many common ideas about grief are actually

fiction. It's not an easy process to change our views but hopefully these sessions will help you tackle these learned ideas.

Thanks so much for participating today. After each session, a box will pop up with two questions. Feel free to answer! All your answers are private and will be sent to me directly.

How do you feel after this session?
What have you taken away from this session?

Chapter Nine

Later that day

When I get home, Tolani is heaping spaghetti into a bowl and covering it with the rich Bolognese from the pot on the stove. Grandma is snoring loudly on the sofa. Tolani is wearing a fitted blazer with smart trousers and her hair is parted to the side, so she must've just come back from her uni work placement.

'Do you want some?' Tolani asks. She's already spooning some into a bowl for me.

'Thanks, Tolly.' My stomach grumbles and my mouth waters as she hands me the bowl and we go to sit down at the table.

Between mouthfuls, Tolani asks, 'Soo . . . how's the support group going?'

I shrug.

Tolani pauses with the fork in her hand. 'That's it? You don't have anything else to say? Sadé, you can talk to me about it, you know.'

I focus on chewing and swallowing while I think. 'I know,' I reply. 'It's just . . .'

'Just what?'

I sigh. 'The support group can be confusing. Like they keep on asking me how I feel, and I dunno.'

My feelings curl and twist, tangling up my mind. How can it be right? The pain feels like it's going to blast my brain, all my energy drained. How can it be right? It makes night merge with mornings and has me yawning. How can it be right?

Tolani sticks the fork into her food. 'Feel however you want to, Sadé.'

After that last session, my insides felt shredded like grated cheese. *Could what I think is fact really be fiction?*

Picking her fork back up, Tolani takes another bite and starts talking about something else, but my mind is still on the support group. Ellie says that everyone grieves in different ways. So why do I feel like this is another thing I'm no good at?

Tolani puts her bowl in the sink to soak and sits back down, opening her olive-green backpack. 'All right, I need to get some work done.'

Leaving Tolani, I walk upstairs. As I stand outside Mum's study door, my throat tightens like the lid of jam that's been in the fridge for ages. Didn't Ellie say all feelings are OK? That it was important to combine the person with the experience. *It's important to bring the two together, like a sandwich, and find ways to deal with these emotions.*

I hear the front door open and close downstairs. Teni is home from school.

ZOMBIE SLAYERS! (AND FUNMI)

Funmi: @sadé where did you go at lunch

Alfie: yh

thought we were gonna play another game

Me: library

Funmi: to do mrs karoma's work?

I wrote an essay

have you given yours in?

Me: I forgot!!! I'll give it

in tomorrow before maths

Alfie: mine is a story of about my hero beating a monster called Freddy 🙂

I put my phone away and stare at Mum's door again. Taking a deep breath, I nudge open the study door. The faded smell of peppermint tea hits my nose. Dad's 'Best Dad' mug rolls on to its side. *What is it doing in here?* As I pick up the mug, cold coffee drips on to the floor.

Mum's room is exactly the same. The pinned homemade cards from Mum's Year Three class telling her to 'get well soon' are on the board in front of her writing desk.

The curtains flap – the window is open, which is weird. Leaning over her desk, I shut the window, trapping Mum's peppermint smell in.

Why don't you find a time to do something in memory of your mum?

I take my purple journal out of my bag and flip to a poem I've just started. With my legs pulled up under me, I close my eyes and open them in my world.

* * *

Vines grow behind me. First, white orchids grow, making

a comfy base, then the armrests, until I'm sitting on a wide green throne in the middle of the Sanctuary.

The tall, arched stone structures create shadowy coverings. Lilac light peeks through the cracks in the walls.

I picture what this place used to be like before I spoiled it. Moths zooming down the stone corridors and through the stone arches. It used to be buzzing with animals. Giant floral birds with bodies made of orchids, bellflowers and daffodils; their curved necks pecked at the moss growing on the walls. My stone sanctuary.

'Mum,' I whisper. 'Where'd you go?'

Nix's soft head nudges my foot.

I remember one of the questions at the end of the support group. *How do you feel after this session?*

'A mouthy, slithering snake of a question.

Feelings wriggling in their holes

Words can't fill.

They're leaking every day

but time won't heal.

How do you feel after this session?

A poisonousness toad of a question.

Feelings cut me.

The pain is leaking memories I can't keep—'

'Pssst, Sadé,' one of the orchids interrupts me, craning her stem. 'I heard from the tulips that the rapping roses are looking for you. It's important.'

'Thanks!'

I rush down the stone corridor and out of the Sanctuary and hop on the four-leaf-clover-shaped stepping stones, cross the swaying vine bridge and rush through the Gardens until I reach my rapping roses.

'Something important we gotta tell you,' Monica sighs.

Savannah's yellow bud trembles as she speaks. 'Listen to what we have to say, they want to kill us and get us out of the way.'

'Who?' I ask. 'Who wants to?'

Keith's blue bud bends from left to right before he whispers, 'Sadé. We don't know but something ain't right here. There's something evil in here with us.'

'Evil like what?'

Savannah's petals quiver. 'It's the silence and the red snake eyes.'

'The claws. The growls,' Monica says.

Oh no. Not growls. I heard them in the classroom and coming from the bushes!

'We're scared. It's not safe here any more!' Keith shouts.

This world is bad because of me, and I'll do anything to save it. Plucking a blade of grass from the ground, I trap it between my thumbs and blow.

A swarm of muttering moths answer my call.

'Skeweeeee?' they ask in unison.

'I called because I want you to protect the rapping roses. And tell me if you see *anything*. Can you do that?'

'Bleee,' they respond.

'Thanks. I'm going to fix this. I promise—'

* * *

'Shadz!' Teni shouts. 'I'm talking to you.'

My eyes pop open and I swivel the chair round to face the door, my heart hammering in my chest. Teni is standing in front of me, flipping her long braids. She's still in her school uniform.

What did I do now?

'I asked you why you're in here.'

My neck feels as hot as an iron. 'Why can't I be in here?'

Teni closes the study door behind her. 'Cos it's Mum's room. It needs . . .' Teni's shoulders droop. 'It just needs to stay the same. I don't even know why I'm shouting at you. Sorry. But what *are* you doing in here?'

'I miss Mum.'

Teni flops into Mum's purple reading chair at the back of the room. She brings her legs up and plays with the gold anklet Mum bought her.

'Do you remember when Mum used to leave little notes in our bags?' she asks.

I smile. 'Yeah, she left me short stories.'

Mum's stories will always be the best.

'And that one time I was obsessed with that cartoon.' Teni snaps her fingers together. 'Man . . . what was the name of it again?'

Tolani pushes open the door and answers. '*The Amazing Adventures of Brady*.'

'That's it!' Teni yells. 'She made me a Brady cake from scratch.'

Tolani sits down on the floor, leaning her head back against one of the desk legs. 'I remember when I was *so* stressed about my homework being neat. I messed it up so many times, but Mum stayed up with me all night until I finished it.' She laughs. 'Can you believe the teacher didn't even check the homework in the end?'

We all laugh.

'So . . . Grandma is going back to Nigeria soon,' Tolani sighs. 'I think it'll be nice for us to do something together before she leaves. We can take her out to a restaurant as a family.'

Teni's legs drop to the floor. 'Yeah, we should. But I'm not going to that *disgusting* restaurant down the road. What's it called again? They have the deadest food.'

'What about Golden Dragon?' I offer, already smelling the sweet, sticky ribs and the egg fried rice.

We haven't been there since Mum died.

My sisters are staring at me with smiles on their faces. 'What?' I ask.

'You and that restaurant, Sadé,' Tolani laughs. 'OK, I'll book us a table. Do you still want me to look over your essay, Teni?'

'Yeah,' Teni replies, 'but remember I have to hand it in tomorrow so you're only checking for spelling and grammar – that's it.'

'Why are you looking at me like that?' Tolly asks.

Teni opens the door and turns back. 'Because you're always doing the most.'

Tolani huffs. 'There's a reason I get Firsts in my uni essays, you know . . .'

My sisters' voices fade away as they head downstairs. I pick up my journal from the floor. Talking about memories and Mum reminds me of a time when colours were surging and spinning, swaying in a place where there was no hurting. Picking up my pen, I turn to a new page and write:

> No hurting, no pain lurking ready to
> pounce, leaving me without control and I'm
> spinning out. If I'm Earth, my chest is the
> moon too far away to connect to – I'm
> hovering between the two.

Part Two

Chapter Ten

Wednesday

My backpack bangs against my back as I rush to Mrs Karoma's room. I want to hand in my homework before Mr Sanders's lesson starts.

Looking through the classroom window, Mrs Karoma is seated at her desk, typing on her computer. I knock on the door and she calls out, 'Come in, Sadé.'

I enter the room and dig through my bag, take out the poem that I wrote and place it on her desk. 'Here is my homework, miss. I'm sorry for handing it in so late.'

'Well, I *did* say before next lesson, which is tomorrow.' Mrs Karoma reaches for the paper and says excitedly, 'I can't wait to read it.'

'Thanks, miss. I have to go, or I'll be late.'

'Go, go. Don't let me keep you.'

I sprint down the blue corridor all the way to the yellow corridor, where my maths lesson is, and join the line. The poster on the wall beside me is counting down to the official talent show auditions at the end of next week. If my words really are coming back to me, maybe I can audition after all.

'Inside, quickly and quietly,' Mr Sanders says.

We file inside. He stands at the front of the classroom, straightens his tie and pulls down on his mustard sweater vest, then clears his throat.

'We're going to change the layout for this lesson and have some fun.'

Mr Sanders thinks multiplication is fun. He bounces forward and backward on the balls of his feet. 'We're going to play . . . "Coordinates Battleship".'

'Battleship?'

'What's that, sir?'

'Do you think we're pirates, sir?'

Mr Sanders hisses. 'If you'd be quiet for a second and listen, then you would know what Coordinates Battleship is.'

Alfie narrows his eyes and pulls his jumper down so that it covers the top of his trousers like Mr Sanders's. Nudging him, I try not to laugh so we don't get in trouble – that's the last thing we need.

'For this game you will be working in pairs.'

The noise rises as everyone gets excited and start whispering about who they're going to work with.

'You will choose your partner randomly from the bowl.'

Moans and groans come from all directions. Mr Sanders strides down the centre of the room with a clear bowl in his hands.

Funmi mumbles a prayer. 'In Jesus's name.' She plucks a piece of paper from the bowl and waves it at Simone.

Callum gets Alfie.

Jas stirs her tan-brown hand in the bowl and pulls a piece out. Trina reads the paper and sniggers before looking at me. Jas picks up her tiny school bag and moves to the seat beside me. My stomach fizzes like a shaken bottle of Fanta.

'Here are the rules. Each pair will be given a grid like this . . .' Mr Sanders holds up a sheet. 'We're revising what you've already learned on coordinates. But making it competitive!'

Mr Sanders switches on his speakers and battle music blasts through the room as he nods off beat, shuffling along and clapping his hands. As my eyes meet Jas's, we burst out laughing like old times and she hides behind her long, tight brown curls.

'Good luck, everyone. And there's a prize for the winners!' Mr Sanders bellows over the music.

'Is it maths books again, sir?' Alfie asks. 'No one wants that.'

The class mumbles in agreement.

'No,' huffs Mr Sanders. 'Even though all of you should be grateful because those books are of the highest quality. However, *this* prize is of the sweet and cavity-inducing kind.'

'We have to win, Cal,' Alfie stresses.

'And any pair who fail to work well together will automatically get a lunchtime detention today,' Mr Sanders barks.

I push the paper over to Jas and murmur, 'Where do you wanna put the first symbol?'

Jas takes two pencils out of her pencil case and hands me one. She slides her finger with its clear nail polish over the sheet. 'Hmmm, I don't know anything about strategy so I think we should just put the special symbols . . . anywhere.'

We draw the symbols in random boxes – crossbones, two swords, a treasure chest, and some other pirate stuff.

Mr Sanders calls, 'I hope everyone is ready. Starting from the x axis, five across and six up . . .'

Working with Jas reminds me of when we used to spend hours together at my house. One minute we were in Year Seven and close friends; the next, she didn't talk to me any more and she was best friends with Trina. Trina is the worst.

Callum fidgets in his seat with his right hand raised. 'Sir, sir! We landed on the sword. What does that mean?'

'Arr!' Mr Sanders slashes his hand through the air. 'It means that you can cut your neighbours' score in half.'

Callum high-fives Alfie and turns to Funmi. 'Mwahahahaha.'

Funmi crosses her arms. 'Oh my days, it's not fair. We're winning!'

'All's fair in love and war,' Mr Sanders replies.

'Ha ha,' Alfie teases her. 'You lose. We win.'

Funmi pushes him gently. 'Cheater.'

Mr Sanders frowns as his fun battery runs out. 'Do you both want detentions?'

Their mouths close quicker than a Venus flytrap.

'Sir, there's only, like, two minutes until the lesson's done.' Simone points at the red triangle-shaped clock on Mr Sanders's desk.

'You're right. Thanks, Simone,' he replies. 'Pass all your sheets to the front and I will tell you who the winners of Coordinates Battleship are.'

The ringing bell shakes the classroom as bags bash on desks and voices rise. Mr Sanders raises a single sheet in the air with an oily smile on his splotchy face. 'And the winners are . . . Trina and Freddy.'

What?

'Here is your prize,' Mr Sanders says, handing them the red Celebrations carton. 'Make sure you don't eat any chocolates during your lessons this afternoon. Off to lunch!'

Trina walks over to Jas, pretending I'm not here. 'Did you see we won? I'm like a maths genius. Are you ready for lunch?'

Holding up Jas's pencil, I say, 'Thanks for lending it to me. Alfie never gives my pencils back.'

Trina wrinkles her creamy, freckled nose. 'Ew, I wouldn't take it, Jazzie. You might catch something from her.'

Jas looks at Trina and then back at the pencil before taking it. 'You're welcome, Sadé.' She tilts her head. 'This doesn't make us friends again though, in case that's what you thought.'

Trina makes a fake sad face. 'Look at her, Jazzie. I think she's going to cry.'

Trina links arms with Jas, pulling her away. 'Let's go before we miss the hot food.'

The pressure in my throat builds, until I can't breathe properly. I shove my maths book into my bag and the corner rips against the zip as I tug it closed.

'Where are you going?' Funmi asks.

I race out of the room and keep on running to the red corridor. Using the back of my hand, I wipe the hot tears off my face. The toilet door has a 'Locked for maintenance'

sign on it, but when I push on the door, it opens. Everyone avoids this toilet because the soup of smells inside are deadly. My shoes stick to the floor like paste as I slip into the last cubicle with an 'Out of order' note on it. No one will look in here. I hold my breath and use a piece of tissue to lower the toilet lid down.

It only feels like ten seconds have passed before the bathroom door swings open. Shoes echo from outside the cubicle. I step on to the toilet seat and crouch down.

'Sadé,' Funmi calls. 'Are you in here?'

I keep very still.

Funmi looks under the cubicles. 'I don't think she's in here, Alfie,' she sighs. 'Let's try the toilets on the green corridor.'

As the bathroom door clicks shut, a burning sweet and salt popcorn smells clogs my nose, until I'm coughing. A swarm of butterflies hover in front of me, flickering between jet black and shimmering gold before they change into a shape of a claw and then they disappear.

The door creaks open again.

Did my friends come back to look for me?

A scratching sound makes me cup my ears. It's as if nails are being dragged across the wet floor.

BANG!

One of the toilet doors flies open.

BANG!

There are four toilets and I'm in the last one.

BANG!

I jump backwards and my foot catches the toilet flush. It keeps on flushing and doesn't stop.

The slow, scratching noise is back. A large shadow appears under my door, and then two huge marigold claws which look like cracked earth without water.

'He-hen? How?' I splutter, trying to make sense of it all. 'How are you here? How are you in this world?'

We'll be seeing you soon.

'We couldn't stay in your world,' she clucks roughly. 'So we've come here instead.'

The hairs on the back of my neck stand up.

Someone laughs outside the toilets and the claws vanish. Slowly, I open the door, peering out to see if Hen is still in here, but she's gone.

Chapter Eleven

I'm so busy running from the toilets that I almost bash into Mr Sanders, who looks unhappy to see me.

'No running in the corridor,' Mr Sanders snaps. 'You should know this, Sadé. Why were you running?'

I take deep breaths, trying to stop my heart from beating right out of my chest, but it's not working and dark spots dance in front of my eyes.

'It's n-nothing, sir.'

'Hmmm. Well then.' Mr Sanders rocks forwards with his arms crossed behind his back. 'I'm guessing you're here for the maths Learning Lab.'

Mr Sanders points to the red door that we're standing outside. I'd forgotten all about the Learning Lab. I *did* tell Ellie I would try.

'Yes, sir.'

'Good,' he replies, before stalking off down the corridor.

Peering inside the Learning Lab, I look out for marigold

claws, listen for growling, or anything else strange. I inhale, just in case the burnt popcorn smell is back.

'Hey! First time here?'

I shriek, jumping in the air with my bag clutched to my chest. The voice belongs to an upper-schooler with black hair tied into two buns. She pops her gum and points to a piece of paper on the table. 'Sorry, didn't mean to scare you. Sign in there. You'll be with Sunny.'

'Yo, newbie!' another upper-schooler shouts from the corner of the classroom. 'You're with me.'

I shuffle in between the tables like I'm walking through the maze in the Gardens.

As I reach Sunny, the last corner of a tuna and sweetcorn sandwich disappears into his mouth. He wipes the escaped mayo from his lip.

I stand by the chair opposite him, not wanting to sit down.

'Maths isn't *that* scary.' He chuckles. 'Trust me, man. Take a seat and be prepared to be trained by the master.'

Raising his arms, Sunny chucks the sandwich wrapper across the room, aiming for the bin, but the wrapper bounces off the edge and hits another student walking past.

'Whoops! Sorry.'

I put my hand to my mouth, trying not to laugh.

Sunny pushes his square, black-rimmed glasses up his nose with his non-mayo finger. He has thick black eyebrows which match his cropped hair and contrast with his sand-coloured skin.

'What do you need help with?'

Everything.

'Okaaay. Not a talker, I see.' Sunny taps the table with a pen. 'You got your maths book?'

I slide it across the table, my hand shaking a bit because he's going to see how bad I am at maths.

They're all going to know. Leaving me exposed like the cap off a felt-tip pen till I'm dry and washed out.

With one hand, Sunny flips my book open to the first page, my rubbish quizzes on display like a dress on a mannequin.

'Sadé,' he says, reading my name off the front of the book. 'I can work with this. They don't call me the master for nothing.'

'Who calls you that?' I ask.

Sunny pushes his glasses up his nose again with a chuckle. 'People.' He taps my maths book. 'Two things. You're getting confused with the basics, *and* you have Mr Sanders.'

'He's the worst,' I mutter.

'That's what she said.' He double-taps the table like a drum and hisses like a cymbal.

'Who said?' I ask. 'Who's she?'

Sunny's lips part as he stares at me. 'It was a *joke*. You ever heard of one of them?'

'Uhh yeah, but aren't jokes supposed to be funny?'

'He he ha ha,' Sunny replies with a face as straight as a ruler. 'Anyways, you've got *me* to help you with maths now.' Sunny pops his collar.

'So, if you help me, I *can* get better?' I ask.

'Yeah, course. Maths is all in the technique. It's nothing like English. Writing. Words. Blah, blah, blah. Shakespeare. Yeah, no one cares.'

My shoulders draw back. 'I like English and words *and* writing.' *And if I write something good enough in my new journal maybe I'll be able to audition for the talent show.*

'Oh, so you're one of them,' Sunny smirks. 'I won't hold it against you, and I'll have you acing these quizzes.'

My skin tingles. If I can do well, then no one needs to worry about me. If I can get good grades, my world might get better.

Zigzagging between students, Funmi, Alfie and I battle to get to science. The corridors are as packed as the food market on Saturdays, where people bump into each other, trying to buy the ripest fruits and vegetables.

'I can't believe Jas said that to you. Why would you

want to be friends with her now anyways?' Funmi says. 'She's *so* rude now. Trina is making Jas as evil as she is!'

I'd almost forgotten the whole thing happened because I was running from gloomy Hen, but I can't tell my friends about gloomy Hen. I don't want them to feel scared like I do.

'Anyway, can we get chicken and chips after school?' Funmi asks us.

'Yeah!' me and Alfie shout in unison, and I start feeling better.

A boy from our class walks towards us and stops Alfie. 'Alfie, mate, you got any more of those sour sweets?' he asks, digging in his pocket.

'Yeah, they're a pound.'

Looking around first, Alfie pulls open his blazer to show his inside pockets which are lined with sweets, crisps and chocolates.

Alfie gives the boy a pack of sweets and takes the pound coin.

'If a teacher catches you, you're going to be in so much trouble, Alfie,' Funmi warns.

'I'm not gonna get in trouble and I'm only doing this cos it's Hailey's birthday soon and I need to get her a present.'

Hailey is Alfie's younger sister, and he would do *anything* for her – like my sisters would do for me.

'Why are my feet wet?' Funmi asks, lifting her dripping black leather shoes. 'These are new.'

The entire red corridor is flooded. A lower-schooler jumps up and down, splashing the murky water on her friends.

Mrs Williams's red wellies match the colour of her face as she tramps down the corridor with the janitor rushing beside her. We call him Mumbling Ted because he always mumbles when you ask him anything.

'Move back to the walls, everyone!' Mrs Williams yells. 'Where is it coming from?'

Ted mumbles something.

'Did you say it's coming from the toilets?' she asks. 'But those toilets were supposed to be locked for maintenance!'

I freeze.

Funmi and Alfie share a look because those toilets weren't locked, but they don't know that I was in there.

Pulling a huge set of keys out of his forest-green overalls, Mumbling Ted's fingers fumble as he tries to find the right key. Shoving him out of the way, Mrs Williams pushes the door open and brown-tinged water rushes over her feet.

'Well, *clearly* it wasn't locked, was it?'

Mumbling Ted holds up a long silver rusty key.

'Ted!' Mrs Williams screams.

He mumbles.

'I don't care if it's coming from the last cubicle – just *fix it*!'

The last cubicle – that's where I was hiding. My foot had hit the toilet flush, but I thought it would eventually stop flushing. I look down to avoid Alfie's and Funmi's eyes.

'Everyone to your lessons, now!' Mrs Williams bellows.

As soon as the last bell rings for the day, I'm the first one out of the door with my bag bouncing on my back. I need to get away from school today.

'Sadé, why are you running off?' Funmi calls. 'I thought we were getting chicken and chips.'

'We can get Morley's tomorrow.'

'All right, but you're getting me an extra BBQ wing.'

I smile. 'Deal!'

As the front door slams behind me, Grandma peeks her head over the sofa. 'Bawo ni ile-iwe ṣe wa looni?'

'School was good, Grandma.'

Jas was old Jas and then went back to new Jas. Somehow Hen was in the real world and now school is swimming in toilet water.

I rush up the stairs and lock the bedroom door behind me. Before I can even drop my bag on the floor, my eyes close, and I'm pulled into my world.

* * *

Nix is waiting for me on the cliff. Her high-pitched squeal pierces the air. As I try to pat her head, Nix nips at my hand with her beak.

'Ouch, Nix!' I shout, massaging my hand. 'Why'd you bite me?'

She flaps her wings and lowers her soft bulky body for me to climb on. As we dive off the cliff, Nix loops around my world, squealing. She twirls around some vines and through the broad oak swing. Nix's wings beat fast as she heads towards the Word Tunnel.

'Nix. Slow down!'

I'm frightened that we're going to hit the side of the tunnel. She squeals again. Lowering her head and flattening her wings, she shoots through the tunnel like a bullet and my stomach spins. The words blur in front of me. I shut

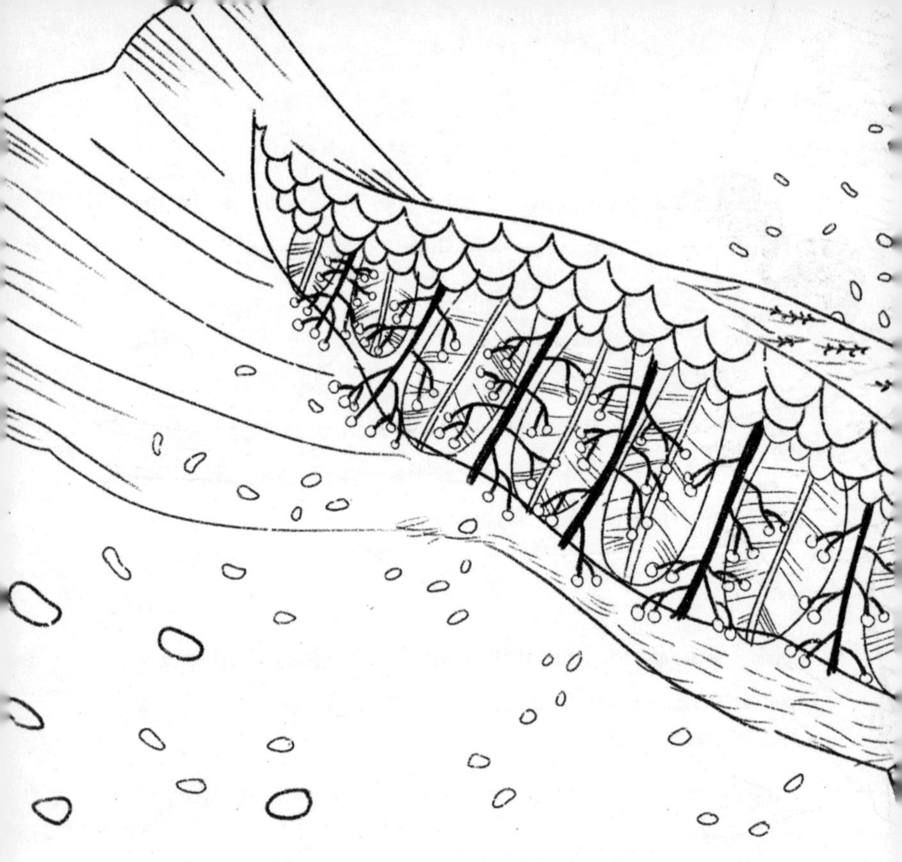

my eyes until I feel the fresh breeze on my face again.

We're out of the tunnel. Nix skids to a stop outside the Sanctuary. Dizzy, I climb off her back and the world rotates around me as I find my balance. Nix lowers her head and covers her face with her wing.

Two tall palm trees on either side of the Sanctuary's high-arched stone doorway bow to make an entrance for us to walk through. Vines sliver over the walls.

Nix squeals again. As I follow her down the stone corridor, there's a crunch under me. Lifting up my foot,

purple goo from the ground clings to it. A transparent wing with a purple trim twitches. Butterfly bodies litter the stony ground.

Crouching down, blood rushes to my ears. One of the wings rests in my palms. *Who would kill them?*

Chapter Twelve

Thursday

Mrs Karoma's words swerve around the classroom, but I can't concentrate on them or on *A Midsummer Night's Dream*. I can't stop thinking about Hen escaping to the real world and the butterfly bodies in my world.

'What worser place can I beg in your love –

And yet a place of high respect with me –

Than to be used as you use your dog?'

Alfie pants. 'Woof! Woof!'

Simone giggles, patting him on the head. 'Good boy.'

Mrs Karoma cackles. 'Thanks, Simone and Alfie. Jasmine, please continue.'

'Tempt not too much the hatred of my spirit. For I am sick when I do look on thee,' Jas reads.

'Helena loves him *so* much, that it's an honour just to be treated the way he would treat a dog,' Mrs Karoma explains. 'In response, Demetrius says that looking at Helena makes him feel sick. Let's end the lesson with some insults. Turn to your partner on the left and practise with the words on the board.'

Why left? Why not right? Alfie is on my right, but Trina is on my left. Free pick 'n' mix sweets vs broccoli for a year.

'Urgh,' Trina groans. 'I guess I'm stuck with you then.'

I don't want to be stuck with broccoli either.

'Oi!' Alfie shouts at Simone. 'You're a purpled onion-eyed codpiece!'

The anger that I'd kept jammed inside from finding my dead butterflies springs out. 'Thou rank, paper-faced pigeon egg.'

Trina blinks a few times, surprised, before saying, 'Thou *puny*, pinch-spotted malt-*worm*.'

'Thou *hideous*, lily-livered hugger-mugger.'

'Thou . . . thou greasy, ill-bred mould toad,' Trina stammers.

'Thou puny, empty-hearted lout.'

A slow, nasty smile creeps on Trina's face and she lowers her voice so only I can hear her. 'You stupid loser.'

I flinch. Those words aren't on the board, but it doesn't matter because bullies destroy, uproot, their vines choking lives so we can't shoot.

'There's a Shakespearean deep inside all of you, that's for sure! Pack away, please,' Mrs Karoma declares. 'I'll be coming round to hand back your Anti-Bullying Week pieces. There is some great work.'

I don't bother looking at the marked homework Mrs Karoma puts on my desk because my words have created nothing but trouble lately. What's the point?

'Brilliant, brilliant work, Sadé,' Mrs Karoma beams. 'I *knew* you had it in you.'

I look at the comment she left on my work.

This is amazing, Sadé! I love the imagery and how you showed the effects of bullying. Go and see your work at reception!

She's obviously got my paper switched with someone else's. I look closer. My words are right there on the page.

'Actually, Sadé, can you wait behind, please?' Mrs Karoma asks. 'Everyone else is free to go to lunch.'

Funmi is already halfway out the door. 'Sadé, meet us at the field. We'll be practising the dance.'

Mrs Karoma waits until everyone has left before she talks. 'I just wanted to say well done again. I didn't know you were a poet.'

Me? A poet?

'Thanks, miss, but I'm not a poet.'

Her bangles jingle as she waves her hands in the air. 'Don't be so modest, Sadé. I know a poet when I see one. If you're interested, the English Literature Club meet after school. We have a meeting today, in fact. Come and pay us a visit if you have time. With your talent, you have a great chance at the auditions for the talent show. Think about it.'

I nod and shuffle to the door.

'Oh, and Sadé, if there's ever a time you need to speak to someone about anything going on at school – or anyone . . .' Her eyes drift to Trina's seat. 'Come and find me. Now, I need some lunch. If you have time, stop by reception and see your work on display.'

'I will, miss. Thanks, miss.'

The Anti-Bullying display takes up half the wall behind reception where Chris is sitting.

'Hi, Sadé. Are you here for the box?' he asks, reaching down for it.

'No, I'm here to, erm, see my work.' I point to the display behind him.

Chris beams at me as he straightens papers on his already spotless desk. 'That's great.'

There's a large tree with branches snaking along the wall with the chosen pieces of creative writing hanging off the branches like fruit. I can't take my eyes off the one in the centre, in a gold frame. Mine. I can't believe *my* work is at reception.

My eyes drift to the talent show audition sign-up clipboard, which is now under the Anti-Bullying display.

Remembering what Mrs Karoma just said, and before I change my mind, I bend down and write my name slowly, curving the e.

Part Three

The Explosion

Chapter Thirteen

Friday

'What film did you watch?' Alfie asks Funmi.

'That scary one on Netflix everyone is talking about,' she answers. 'I used my brother's account, but it gave me nightmares. My dream was like *The Hunger Games*.'

'I dreamed that I was swimming in KFC,' Alfie snorts. 'When I woke up, there was only soggy cornflakes for brekkie, and Levi stuck his hands in my bowl.'

Funmi looks like she's going to be sick. 'You still ate the cereal, didn't you?'

Alfie rubs his stomach with a playful grin on his face. 'Yup.'

We're wading through the crowd of people in the red corridor to get to science. Because the floor is covered in plastic, our feet squeak noisily. Mumbling Ted passes us with a fresh carton of red paint for the walls as it's started peeling off.

'Did you hear that there's a ghost in there now?' Alfie

asks, pointing to the toilet door.

'I heard that too,' Funmi agrees.

It was *definitely* not a ghost in there.

'8E!' Mr Andrews, our science teacher, bellows.

He's standing outside the lab in one of those long, white coats and goggles. 'I'm out of chemistry jokes, but I should *zinc* of a new one. Jasmine and Trina. You can head in and set up for your presentation.'

I follow the others into the lab. With a bad report hanging over my head, I need our science presentation to go well too – at least we're not doing it today.

'When we do ours, it's going to be better than theirs,' Funmi assures me. 'We can practise again when you come to my house today.'

'Before Jas and Trina get started, I just want to remind the class that for your science presentations, you will be marked as a group and get feedback individually too. Make sure you try your best.' Mr Andrews signals to Jas and Trina. 'Take it away, ladies.'

Trina's smile is as sweet as poison ivy. 'Hey, everyone!'

'Hi, Trina,' the class calls back.

'Hi, Trina,' Alfie mimics.

Jas clears her throat. 'Hey, everyone. We're going to talk to you about acids, bases and alkalis.'

'There are different types of acids, like dilute acids,'

Trina continues. 'You might have seen this symbol before.' Trina snaps her fingers at Jas like she's her servant and Jas hurries to change the PowerPoint slide. *Why is she friends with Trina?*

A red warning symbol pops up on the screen. 'This warning symbol means that you have to be careful because the acid could irritate your skin.'

Mr Andrews nods in agreement and makes some notes.

'There are also concentrated acids and weak acids, like vinegar, fizzy drinks and tea,' Trina continues. 'Our experiment will demonstrate how much acid everyday fizzy drinks have in them – you'll be amazed!'

At the end of the presentation, the class claps and Mr Andrews says, 'And *that's* how it's done. Well done, ladies.'

Trina and Jas return back to their seats.

'Now, we need some volunteers to hand out the equipment for the experiment. Who wants to help?'

A few hands shoot up, including mine because everyone knows that the more you do, the better your report will be. My fingers wiggle in the air.

'Hmmm. We had Steven and Tracy last time so . . . let's go with Callum and . . . Sadé.'

'Ours was the best. Watch, Jazzie. We're going to get the best grade,' Trina hisses. 'Why are you making that face, Sadé?'

'I wasn't making a face,' I reply.

'Yeah, you were.' Trina looks at Jas. 'Wasn't she, Jazzie?'

My eyes connect with Jas's, and she tugs at her ear, so I *know* she's about to lie.

Jas whispers. 'Yeah?'

'Just leave Sadé alone,' Funmi replies.

'All I was saying, *Fun-me*, is that our presentation will be better than yours. Jazzie, didn't you tell me before that Sadé isn't smart?'

Jas stares at Trina and then at me, before answering. 'I didn't *actually* say that. I said that you weren't good—'

'That you're not good at *anything*,' Trina finishes.

It's your fault, Sadé, because you're no good.

The words clench my heart like a fist.

'Sadé, don't listen to her.' Funmi's voice sounds like it is trapped in a tunnel, like that day in the hall. 'Our experiment is going to be amazing.'

'Lab coats and goggles on,' Mr Andrews calls. 'As you can see, the lab has already been covered with plastic in case things get messy.'

Chairs scrape back as everyone runs to grab the nicer lab coats and goggles, but I can't stop the words.

You're not good at anything.

'Callum, please hand out the observation sheets and,

Sadé, you can help me with the equipment in the side room.'

'Sir, sir. Where are the rest of the coats?' someone asks.

Mr Andrews lets out a sharp breath. 'Hang on! I'm sorry, Sadé, I'll come and help you in a second. Can you put a can of Coke, baking soda and a labelled beaker on each tray, please? I've already put the rest of the materials out. I'll go and deal with this.'

I hop down from my high-up chair and head to the side room where the stacked trays are. As the door closes behind me, butterflies appear out of thin air, shifting into the shape of a scary-looking tiger, with sharp teeth and red eyes.

A deep growl fills the small, tight box room. It's the same strange growl I heard from the bushes that day. It's close. Very close.

Drip.

I turn.

Two red bloodshot snake eyes focus on me from across the room.

'T – Tiger,' I whisper.

Drip.

We'll be seeing you.

Purple goo leaks from the edge of Tiger's long sharp black claws and splatters on the floor. Her mouth is smeared with the purple goo too – the blood of the butterflies. My heart sinks. Tiger was the one who killed them. The Tiger I knew only ever cared about creatures. As her dark sinister form creeps closer, I move, and the edge of the tray digs into my back.

'Isn't this a quaint little gathering,' Fox says, nestled in the corner of the room.

Tiger turns her head towards Fox and growls at him for interrupting. Fox pins me with his glowing orange orbs and treads closer.

Beads of sweat form around my eyebrows. 'I – I'm going to fix it. My grades . . . they're getting better. I swear.'

'What do you swear on?' Fox asks, baring his thin teeth.

'Isn't it your fault that your mum didn't get better?'

Drip.

Fox's eyes flash and Tiger slams her large black form into the table, knocking a few of the cans of Coke over. Her ears twitch and point up like horns, before both creatures disappear into thin air.

Crouching on the floor, I pick the cans up to put them back on to the desk and stand up. The door swings open.

'Sorry about that,' Mr Andrews says, keeping the door held open with his foot. 'Let's get these out there.'

He quickly takes the cans from the desk and puts them on the trays. I can't tell which were the ones that fell on the floor.

'Wait, Mr Andrews, some of the cans fell down and got shaken up.'

The noise of talking from the other side of the classroom drowns my voice. He doesn't hear me.

Mr Andrews leaves the room and I follow him out, hoping that everything will be fine.

It all happens in slow motion. As Jasmine and Trina open their cans, Coke sprays all over them, soaking them both from their hair to their matching shoes.

Gasps and titters spread throughout the room. Trina shouts and trips into Jas, who knocks the equipment on to the floor.

Mr Andrews's hands fumble as he hands over rolls and rolls of tissue. It's a soggy mess.

Dripping with Coke, Trina screams, 'This is all *your* fault, Sadé! I know you shook our cans because you're jealous of us. Didn't she, Jazzie?'

The whole class stares at me, including Mr Andrews.

'It wasn't me,' I whisper. 'I didn't do it.'

They don't believe me.

I have to get out of here.

Chapter Fourteen

The white science coat flaps behind me like a cape as I rush down the empty corridors. Coming out by the side of the sports hall, I push through the bushes at the back where my secret spot is. It's a blue-and-white striped bench, which is always empty.

But today, it's not empty. There is an upper-schooler sitting on my bench. He has brown spikes with two lines shaved at the side of his head and a white untucked shirt. Looking up, he sees me standing there and moves his jumper for me to sit down next to him.

I sit. He leans down to grab a torn talent show poster from the big stack under his white trainers, which are definitely not part of the school uniform. Scrunching it up, he throws the ball of paper through the big hole in the bushes, where it lands beside the bin.

The upper-schooler shoves the stack towards me with his foot and tilts his head at me, suggesting that I do the same. I stare at the pile for a second before I pick one up, smoothing out the poster.

Scrunch. Toss.

'Why you bunking class?' the upper-schooler asks.

Scrunch. Toss.

'I'm not bunking,' I whisper. 'Everyone thinks I shook some Coke cans up on purpose, so this girl would get sprayed.'

Scrunch. Toss.

'Nice. I did that last year in the canteen and Mrs Williams suspended me for, like, three days.'

Am I going to get suspended?

After a while, the upper-schooler says, 'See ya' and wanders off.

Closing my eyes and leaning back on the bench, I imagine my forest. Slowly, it materialises in front of me . . .

* * *

Plucking some grass, I bring my thumbs together and whistle for the moth who read out the tally last time.

'Suppeee dee?' he asks.

'No, I'm not all right. I just saw Tiger,' I whisper. 'It was her who killed those butterflies.'

I whisper it because maybe if I say it quietly enough, it won't be true. The moth flaps around anxiously, before shooting off.

I chase after her deeper into the forest until we get to the Gardens. A frightened crowd of animals and insects surround Nix, who is lying on the grass with emerald-green blood dripping from her leg. If Lion was here, he would've calmed the crowd with a single roar.

'Nix!' I drop down beside her. 'What happened?'

The three rapping roses tremble and their leaves quiver.

'What happened?' I repeat.

Savannah's petals tremor. 'It's the silence and the red snake eyes. She tried to hurt us, but Nix protected us.'

Red snake eyes. 'Was it Tiger?'

Nix makes a sharp, piercing sound and beats her wings against the ground in response.

Two moths whizz off towards the moon pool and return a few minutes later, carrying a large leaf filled with purple water.

'Thanks.' I rub my hands through Nix's petals. 'This might sting a bit, OK?'

Nix nudges my arm with her beak. Slowly, I pour on the water on to the cut, washing away the blood. She flinches, but then keeps still. I carefully place the leaves over the cut and wrap it with a vine.

'Sadé,' Keith whispers. 'What are you gonna do?'

* * *

'What are you doing here, Sadé?' a voice asks.

My eyes pop open and Mrs Williams's denim-coloured eyes glare down at me.

'My office, *now*.'

I follow Mrs Williams to her office in a daze and sit in the chair she points to. She asks me questions which I answer as well as I can. And then she is silent for a long moment.

My eyes are fixed on the painting behind Mrs Williams's desk as she clasps her hands together. 'Mr Andrews confirms what you've told me,' she says at last. 'He believes it was all an accident too. He says that you're a good student and trusts you wouldn't shake up those cans on purpose. But he was worried about you, running off like that.'

'Sorry, miss.' My shoulders slump in relief. I'm not being suspended.

Mrs Williams's desk phone rings and she answers it. 'Hello, Chris. Ah, yes, I'd forgotten. Just give me a minute.' She covers the phone speaker with her hand. 'Sadé, I have to take this call. I don't want to see you skipping class again though.'

'Yes, Mrs Williams.'

As I leave her office, my phone pings with a reminder about my session with Ellie.

ZOMBIE SLAYERS! (AND FUNMI)

Alfie: you OK?

Funmi: sadé??

did you get in trouble?

Trina is saying you did

Me: I'm fine

I'm not in trouble

I might not be in trouble, but I don't know what I'm going to do about the beasts. Opening Ellie's door, I see her fighting with her light-pink knitted scarf. It looks like she has two extra arms. I try not to laugh.

Ellie pauses when she sees me. I dodge the wobbling stack of paper on her desk and hold one side of the scarf as she spins around to free herself.

'Thanks, Sadé,' she says. Her pink fringe is sticking to her forehead. Then she lets out a gigantic yawn. 'Sleep is *very*, very important. I hope you're getting enough sleep. It's important to have your eight hours.' Ellie takes a giant gulp of black coffee from her unicorn mug. 'How is the Learning Lab going?'

Sunny is way better than Mr Sanders already.

'It's good.'

Ellie's cheeks bunch up as she smiles. 'Amazing! I'm glad. Let's talk about the support group. I noticed you contributed much more in the last session. I know it can be difficult sharing with people you don't know. Do you mind if we talk through some of your answers?'

'Do I have a choice?' I mumble. 'Dad says that therapists make you spill all your secrets.'

Ellie makes a funny noise, like a cough is stuck in her throat. 'Who said you don't have a choice? Because of your age, there might be some limitations around choice. Often young people feel excluded around decisions made about them. But you *do* have a choice, Sadé. Life is made up of choices.'

Life is made up of choices. But I didn't have a choice to join this support group or anything else.

We sit in silence for a few minutes.

Ellie starts again. 'As far as your dad's comment goes: I'm a counsellor, not a therapist. And secondly, you tell me only what you're comfortable with. Don't worry, I won't start,' Ellie raises her voice, 'SHOUTING Sadé's business!' She makes herself laugh. 'Seriously, I will never force you tell me anything you're not comfortable with sharing. I just want to know more about what's in that head of yours.'

She smooths out the page. 'So, for the fact and fiction activity, there were two answers I'd like to explore more with you. You said "it is best to stay in control and keep a stiff upper lip" is fact. Tell me a bit more about why you feel this is true'

If I'm not in control, bad stuff happens, like with Mum.

I couldn't control my bad grades, so Mum is gone, my world is weird and those beasts are ruining everything.

'It hurts.' I rest a hand on my stomach.

'Sa-dé.' Ellie's voice is in slow motion.

A round object catches my eye outside Ellie's window. It's a white football. Charlie's blonde ponytail swings as she goes for the ball. Another player kicks her in the leg, and she drops to the ground.

'Sadé, I noticed you were clutching your stomach. Do you get a lot of stomach aches? And other things, like dizziness, sweating and your heart beating fast?'

I nod.

'Do you know what "anxiety" is?'

'Is it like when you're scared?'

'Yes, it has something to do with fear. Anxiety is a feeling of panic or fear about real or imagined threats to us. Imagine a dragon was chasing you—'

'A dragon?'

'Yes. Imagine a dragon chasing you. You get anxious because your body has perceived a threat – the dragon. Your heart is beating faster, sweating and all. To protect you, your brain will tell you to run. It's useful in this situation because it's helping you not get eaten by this dragon. Do you understand?'

'Yeah, I think so.'

'However, there's no dragon chasing you right now. When you imagine the dragon in situations where no real danger exists, then it can impact on your ability to enjoy life and the choices you make. Your heart beats fast, you're sweating, you're scared. An extreme anxious response to this perceived danger would be called a "panic attack".'

She pauses, as though waiting for me to say something, but I sit quietly. She nods.

'People tend to get physical symptoms with their anxiety such as stomach aches. You might not be ready to share with me yet, but we can go through some techniques for when you're feeling anxious. How does that sound?'

No more feeling like my chest is caving in?

'Yeah, it sounds good.'

'Can you place one hand on your stomach just below your ribs?' Ellie asks and demonstrates this for me. 'And the other hand on your chest.'

I copy her. 'Like this?'

'Yes, perfect. Just like that. Now, you're going to inhale for four seconds and hold it in for another four seconds and then exhale for six seconds. Can you try that for me? I'll do it with you.'

I suck in the air, holding and exhaling like Ellie is doing.

'Deep breath in, Sadé, and imagine one of your favourite places.'

Closing my eyes, I picture myself looking out at my beautiful world as it was before it started to change.

After school, I go to Funmi's house with Alfie as she lives near Brandon Estate, where Alfie and me live.

Funmi opens the door and ushers us in. She has changed into a long-sleeved blue denim dress. Funmi has *so* many dresses. Alfie and I are both in blue jeans and a T-shirt under our coats. My T-shirt is yellow with ruffled sleeves and a white daffodil in the centre.

While my house is full of colour and clutter, everything in Funmi's house is pristine and white.

We go into the living room and Funmi tells me what happened after I left science. 'Trina is telling everyone that you sprayed them with Coke on purpose.'

My stomach does a million backflips. *How am I supposed to go back to school on Monday?*

Alfie dives on to the plush white leather sofa like he's swimming. Funmi rushes over to him. 'Alfie, I've told you loads of times. You have to take off your coat, it's got mud on it!'

Alfie flings off his coat, whirling it around in the air, and then swings it around his body. Funmi just stands with her mouth hanging open. I sit on the white leather armchair opposite, trying not to laugh. Alfie can be so silly sometimes!

'Oh, I thought I heard voices,' Funmi's mum says from the doorway.

Alfie quickly folds his coat neatly on his lap.

Funmi's mum matches the house. She's wearing a knee-length white dress and her long, black, straight hair is neat, without one hair out of place.

'Hi, auntie,' I greet her, standing up.

'What did I say about calling me auntie?' she asks with a smile. 'I don't do that outdated "auntie and uncle" business. It's Evelyn.'

She sits down on the arm of the chair and squeezes my hand. 'Sadé, I've missed seeing you around here.' She looks at each of us in turn. 'What are you people up to?'

'We're working on our science presentation,' Funmi exclaims.

Funmi's mum's gaze fixes on the trophy cabinet and goes over to it, fixing the neatly arranged trophies. 'Well, with a brother like yours, you have a tough act to follow.'

She *always* says this. Funmi gets good marks too, and I bet she'll win a trophy for the talent show.

Funmi's smile fades.

'Well, I'll leave you all to it then.'

When Funmi's mum has left the room, Alfie jumps up to distract Funmi. 'I'll start with my bit.' Alfie pulls out his science book and begins reciting from the page. *'The yeast acts as a catalyst, kinda like a helper, to take away the oxygen from the hydrogen peroxide. The yeast contains an enzyme called catalase and enzymes can also be found in potatoes and inside our bodies.'*

Alfie's voice is as boring as Brussels sprouts.

'You have to try and make it sound more interesting,' I exclaim. 'I want us to get a good mark.' I hesitate, then take a deep breath and say it. 'The school sent a letter home about maths.'

Funmi gasps. 'Why?'

I shrug.

'Mr Boring has it in for you.' Alfie frowns. 'It's not fair. Your maths scores are sick.'

Funmi nods so hard that her head looks like it's going to roll off. 'Yeah. I think you should get your dad to talk to Mr Sanders, Sadé. The letter is wrong.'

I can't tell them my dad already knows or how bad I'm really doing. If I try hard enough, and with Sunny's help, my grades will be good and then I won't have to say anything.

'I just want our presentation to go *really* well,' I stress.

'All right. I'll try and make it sound more exciting,' says Alfie. 'Why don't you try reading it, Sadé, to show us?'

Clearing my throat, I imagine myself standing in the middle of my world, reciting my poetry, taking time so the words loop around my tongue. 'This experiment creates a reaction called an exothermic reaction, which means it creates *foam* and *heat*. Once the reaction has finished, you can *feel* the foam and observe the heat created. Now, what are the clues that a chemical change has happened?'

There's a pause. Alfie scratches his head. 'Whoa, that was good, Sadé. You sounded like one of those football commentators!'

'Was it?' I ask, unsure. 'Did I?'

Funmi squeals, 'Yes, Alfie's right. You sounded really confident.'

My stomach bubbles, but this time it's in excitement at my friends' words.

Funmi sits down on the arm of the chair and rests her head against mine, looking at the trophy cabinet again. 'When I'm at dance class, our teacher gets us to practise until we get it right. We can do the same. We'll make sure we get the best grade. Let's go again from the top!'

I stand up and begin speaking. This time I add hand motions as I speak. Before I know it, we're ready for the presentation and I'm not worried any more.

Our presentation is going to be the best.

Chapter Fifteen

It's Saturday morning and my journal is open on my bed. I lie on my stomach scribbling in it.

> Grief is a swear word or haven't they heard? Thrown around like a ball in a game of catch. It's me against grief, but it's not a fair match cos grief is a Casio calculator with all the answers. I'm failing. It's grief this and grief that. Do you want chips and ketchup on the side of that? Grief with a Maccy D's milkshake. Grief with one scoop but no flake. Grief.

The *Deathless 2* app pops up with a game invitation from Alfie. I accept it. While we're having a dance-off with a group of zombies, Alfie messages me.

Alfiedagreatest: let's match up

We do the same dance move at the same time, which freezes the zombies' bodies closest to us and they drop to the ground.

Alfiedagreatest: did u talk to ur dad about mr boring?

Should I tell Alfie the truth about how bad I'm really doing in maths?

Alfie waits at the bottom of the tree while I use my Storm Techs to climb and knock down the special fruit. The higher up the fruit is, the more points you get when you throw it at a zombie.

OnceUponaTime: he knows my maths scores aren't good

Alfiedagreatest: but u got 80% on the quiz

My cheeks burn as I remember the lie that I told Alfie. *Why did I have to lie?*

OnceUponaTime: I got 30%

Alfie's character climbs back down the tree. Then his player puts a hand on my player's shoulder.

Alfiedagreatest: u don't need to lie about ur maths scores
it doesn't matter to me

Later, Tolani trudges into my room dressed in a nice white lace top with black trousers and these large yellow dangling earrings that look like fans hanging off her ears. 'Are you ready to do your hair?'

I drag a chair into the centre of the room. A trail of water drips down my neck, wetting my top.

Tolani touches my very wet afro. 'I'll have to use the hairdryer.' Leaning down, she takes it out of the bottom drawer and unwinds it. 'You know that too much heat isn't good – it can damage your hair. Just think about the breakage as it dries out. It can—'

'Permanently alter its structure and shape,' I finish off.

She stops unwinding the wire and laughs. 'OK, OK! I get it. I just want you to be educated on your hair.'

Tolani hands me the black X-pression hair extensions to hold. She parts my hair down the middle with the pointy comb and spreads warm shea butter on to it. As the heat from the hairdryer touches the top of my ears, I flinch.

'Sadé, stop moving.'

Teni comes into the room and jumps on her grey bedspread. She rests her face in her right palm and plays with her gold hoops, which match the anklet.

Crossing her bare legs, Teni adjusts her short khaki skirt and laughs at a text. Tolani leaves the room to use the toilet so it's only Teni and me left in the room.

Since I told Alfie, I want to be honest about everything. Taking a deep breath, I say, 'Something happened in lesson yesterday.'

Teni rolls over in her bed to face me and puts her phone down. 'What happened?'

All the words come flooding out. 'There's this girl in my class called Trina . . . and she keeps on being mean to me and . . . and saying stuff about me . . . and then there was an accident and these cans got shook up. And Trina thinks I sprayed Coke on them on purpose, but I didn't. It wasn't my fault and now she's telling *everyone* that I did it.'

'What?' Tolani asks, coming back inside the room, frowning. 'Who is this girl? I'm coming down to your school on Monday to sort it out.'

Teni rolls her eyes. 'You don't need to come into school, Tolly,' she says. 'You're too dramatic, man.'

Tolani points at herself. 'Me? I'm *not* dramatic. I just

don't like to hear about someone picking on my little sister. Who does this Trina think she is?'

Teni ignores Tolani and turns to me. 'Don't worry about it, yeah? I'll talk to her at school.'

If I was in my world, I would release the longest ever trail of purple smoke as I let out the breath I'd been holding for weeks. 'Thanks.' *Why didn't I tell my sisters before?*

'Make sure you tell me what happens,' Tolani says. 'Let's finish your hair.'

Once my hair is done, I touch the top of the chunky cornrows with my fingertips. 'Thanks, Tolly.' *I love them.* 'I'll go and see if Grandma is ready to go to Golden Dragon.'

'Ye!' Grandma yells from the living room.

She sounds hurt. Leaping down the stairs, I rush into the living room, my heart hammering against my chest. 'Grandma!'

Grandma is standing with her back to me. She stretches with a grunt. 'Kilode ti apo yii o le pa de?' she mutters.

Why won't this suitcase close?

My heart is still rebounding in my chest like a ping-pong ball. The blood rushes to my ears in a fierce wave and taking breaths gets harder and harder.

Ellie's voice comes into my head. *'Replace negative thoughts with proactive ones.'*

She's fine, Sadé. You didn't do anything to hurt Grandma like you did to Mum.

'Beautiful. This hair really suits you,' Grandma says as she turns to face me and points to one of her overflowing suitcases. 'Wá jókò lórí èyí fún mi.' *Come and sit down on this for me.*

'Thanks, Grandma.' Tiptoeing between open suitcases jam-packed with Primark clothes for family back in Nigeria, I drop down on the biggest suitcase, flattening it with my bum. It's not enough. 'Tolani, Teniola!' Grandma bellows for my sisters. 'Wá k'o jókò lórí apo mi fun mi!'

Come and sit on my suitcase for me.

When Teni sees me perched on the suitcase, she cracks up. Tolani pushes past her. Both of them sit on the suitcase and we squish and squish. Teni falls off the side. Tolani presses hard, until Grandma eventually zips it up.

'O ṣe pupọ.'

Thank you very much.

'I'll go and get Dad,' Tolani offers. 'And then we can go to the restaurant. We can do the rest of the cases when we're back.'

Sandwiched in the middle of the car between Teni and Tolani, I count the colours of the traffic lights all the way to Golden Dragon. I know this route with my eyes closed.

The outside of the building is scarlet with gold Chinese letters right at the top and paper lanterns hanging down from the roof. As we enter the restaurant, a woman at the door greets us. I breathe in the woody incense smell. Lightbulbs sit in white cages on the round wooden tables.

'Welcome to Golden Dragon. I'll take you to your seat.'

As we're being seated, another family is leaving.

'Isn't that your friend?' Teni asks, tilting her chin towards Jas.

Jas turns and her eyes lock with mine. We used to come here all the time for our birthdays. Jas is with her mum,

Ramona, and her baby brother, Ryan.

Ramona's brown ringlet curls shake as she waves at us happily. 'Hi, long time no see. I keep on asking Jasmine why I haven't seen you around in a while, Sadé.' Ryan tugs at her arm. I smile back at her weakly. Luckily, Jas's mum is distracted by Ryan, so she doesn't notice. 'We have to go now but don't be a stranger.'

We're moving towards our table when I hear Jas calling my name. I turn back.

Tucking a bouncy curl behind her ear, she says, 'I know you didn't do the Coke can thing on purpose. I know what Trina said, but I know you didn't do it. You wouldn't do something like that.'

Then Jas hurries out of the restaurant, leaving me standing there with my mouth hanging open.

I think about what Jas said while I'm chewing on the crispy duck, tucking into the delicious special fried rice and slurping on the cold apple juice. I'm still thinking about it when we get back from the restaurant. Once we've zipped up the final suitcase and everyone goes upstairs, it's just Grandma and me.

'Emi yóò sa'aro ẹ pupọ,' she says.

I'm going to miss you so much.

Evil Tiger must've clawed at my chest because it feels raw. 'I'll miss you too. What are we gonna do without you?

Who is gonna wake Teni up for church? Who is gonna do . . .' My throat tightens. *She can't go.*

Grandma cuddles me to her side. 'Omo mi, everything will be well,' she reassures me. 'And trust me, before you know it . . . your dad will be taking you to church.'

I don't know about that.

'Stop worrying, omo mi. Remember that you can't keep things inside. Cast all your burdens upon God.'

I have too many burdens. Too many burdens and too many beasts.

Grandma produces a small square purple box from behind her back and hands it to me.

'Ṣi i,' she urges.

Open it.

I pull at the thin ribbon. It unravels, and I open the lid. Inside is a beautiful gold oval locket with an intricate detail at the front which looks like vines. I open the locket to find a tiny picture of Grandma, Mum and me outside Hope Garden Centre. In the picture, Grandma is mid-sneeze because of all the pollen and Mum is mid-laugh. Her full afro is in a purple ankara headwrap, which matches my purple T-shirt perfectly.

Cherry took the picture. She owns Hope Garden Centre, but I haven't seen her in months.

'Emi yóò wa pẹlu rẹ nigbagbogbo. Yi pada. Yi pada.'

I will always be with you. Turn it over.

Engraved in the gold, there are two words. *Okan mi.*

My heart.

Hugging Grandma, I grip the locket in my hand tightly. 'Thanks, Grandma. I love it.'

Tuesday

Grief Support Group Chat [3]

Ellie[moderator]: Hi everyone. How has everyone's week been?

BendItLikeC: the defender from saint disgusting kicked my leg

You'reDaObiWan4me: LOL saint augustus?

BendItLikeC: that's what I said

Anon05: u get her back?

BendItLikeC: yeah then I got sent off the pitch 😆

You'reDaObiWan4me: lol. my dad paid for this comedy show. my mum took the money back and paid for my sister's science camp

BendItLikeC: LOOL

Anon05: jokes

You'reDaObiWan4me: I'm glad my pain is funny to you

OnceUponaTime: my grandma went home

BendItLikeC: that sucks☹
You'reDaObiWan4me: did she make the best food like my gma?

I smile at my phone because even though she was leaving, Grandma made us a huge pot of her okra soup with beef and fish inside.

OnceUponaTime: the best
Anon05: why is she leaving?

If I could make Grandma stay for ever, I would, but she has to go back. I touch the cold locket pressed against the skin under my jumper. She will always be with me.

OnceUponaTime: she lives in nigeria
she came for mum's funeral and stayed
I'll miss her
Ellie[moderator]: Sorry to hear that your grandma had to leave **@OnceUponaTime.** Change is never easy. We'll be here if you ever want to talk.

Today, we're going to be looking at the signs, emotions and symptoms of grief. I'm going to post a list below. Please feel free to share any that you experienced when your loved one passed away.

Anxiety
Anger
Feeling my friends don't understand
Guilt
Unable to sleep
click for more

BendItLikeC: guilt
wishing things were different
Anon05: angry
BendItLikeC: anger
sad
You'reDaObiWan4me: sick a lot, tired, anxious
Anon05: disappointed
BendItLikeC: sick

As more words pop up on the screen, I'm surprised because I didn't think anyone else felt like I did. I thought those thoughts were only mine.

Ellie[moderator]: Let's pause for a second. Did any of the responses on the list surprise anyone?
Anon05: who wud feel relieved
Ellie[moderator]: There are many reasons why someone would feel relieved.

You'reDaObiWan4me: that's why I didn't put it down

You'd think I'm some serial killer

Ellie[moderator]: would you like to expand on that, @You'reDaObiWan4me?

You'reDaObiWan4me: I felt relieved because my gma died of old age

my gdad didn't

he was sick for a long time

Ellie[moderator]: Sorry to hear about your grandparents. Feeling relief because you don't want your loved one to suffer does not make you bad. In fact, it shows that you have great empathy for others. Does anyone else want to share an emotion about their loved one? It can be anything.

If You'reDaObiWan4me can be so honest, then maybe I can too.

OnceUponaTime: I'm sad my mum will never read to me again

I would've enjoyed that last story, savouring it and letting the warmth fill me like two custard creams dunked in milky tea.

Ellie[moderator]: Thanks for sharing @OnceUponaTime

Anon05: I'm angry at the driver that killed my dad

Ellie[moderator]: If you're feeling angry, there are things that can help. What helps you when you are angry or upset, group?

BendItLikeC: scoring goals

You'reDaObiWan4me: watching comedy specials

Anon05: going to the batting cages

Ellie[moderator]: Thanks for sharing. When we're experiencing such big feelings, it's important that you find ways to cope with these feelings rather than allowing them to sit within us.

Can anyone spot any similarities and differences between your experiences?

You'reDaObiWan4me: @BendItLikeC said they felt sick too

everything made me sick after my gma went

Ellie[moderator]: Thanks @You'reDaObiWan4me Some people who have been bereaved can experience physical symptoms, which are usually temporary. Any other similarities?

BendItLikeC: Me and @OnceUponaTime @Anon05

I was angry too because Tim didn't wait for me

I'm angry that he went in the sea to take a picture

he couldn't swim

angry at myself for being late

Ellie[moderator]: @BendItLikeC You're right to feel whatever you want to feel. You can feel angry. But please don't blame yourself for something you can't control.

BendItLikeC: talking to my friends about it helps sometimes

Would talking to Alfie and Funmi help?

Ellie[moderator]: Yes, sharing with those closest to us can help us process grief. Keep them coming. Post anything else you may have experienced.

My fingers hover over the phone because once it's out there, you can't take it back.

OnceUponaTime: anxious

guilt

scared

Ellie[moderator]: Thanks for sharing @OnceUponaTime. I know it's not always easy to share what you feel, but I just wanted to say this again – all feelings are OK. You may have different feelings at different times and that's OK too. Everyone processes grief differently and one person's grief will never look like another person's.

We're going to look at the five stages of grief now.

Denial, Anger, Bargaining, Depression and Acceptance. I'll take the first one and each of you will take one and then we will discuss responses to them.

Ellie[moderator]: denial – this can't be true

Anon05: anger – why me?

OnceUponaTime: bargaining – I promise to never do anything bad again if they come back

You'reDaObiWan4me: depression – there is nothing left to live for

BendItLikeC: acceptance – I now understand more about my grief

Ellie[moderator]: Has anyone been through any of these stages? Have they been in the same order?
BendItLikeC: anger and bargaining

While the group shares, my conversations with Fox replay in my mind.

'I – I'm going to fix it. My grades . . . they're getting better. I swear.'

'What do you swear on? Isn't it your fault that your mum didn't get better?'

OnceUponaTime: can the stages happen at the same time?
Ellie[moderator]: Yes, the stages can overlap and don't necessarily happen in order. There is no right way to grieve or experience these feelings. Some people don't experience these specific stages at all.
Ellie[moderator]: Once you accept those feelings and understand that your grief is yours, then you can begin to make steps towards coping.

People think that once the stages end, the grieving period is over. But we never really stop grieving. Instead you find new ways to deal with it and even move forwards. The stages become less of a focus and your emotions and acceptance are more prominent. This is why we're here – so you can share and find ways to grow. Can you give me a thumbs-up if you're still with me?

OnceUponaTime: 

Anon05:

You'reDaObiWan4me: 

BendItLikeC: 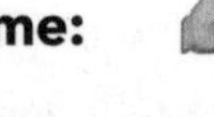

Ellie[moderator]: Before we go, I want to set you a home task for next week. We will be talking about memories. I want you to find something that you think represents your person or a good memory of them and leave it in our drop-off box at reception before the next session. Have a great week, everyone!

Once the chat is done, all I can think about is what BendItLikeC said about sharing stuff with friends helping. Maybe I should tell my friends more, but I don't think I'm ready to talk to them about the support group just yet.

I'm sitting on my bag underneath the stairs that leads to the art rooms. It's one of my favourite secret spots at school. A shadow creeps near, which makes me jump and I bump the top of my head against the bottom of the stairs, sending a sharp pain through my body. I'm scared it's one of the beasts. But it's just the upper-schooler from my secret spot behind the sports hall, looking down at me.

'Whoa, watch out,' he says. 'Are you all right?'

'Yeah,' I reply, rubbing the top of my head.

The upper-schooler throws his baseball in the air and catches it. 'Are you bunking again?'

'No, it's lunchtime,' I reply, picking up my bag. 'And anyways, I'm never leaving lesson again. Mrs Williams caught me.'

'What?' Groaning, he covers his face with his hands. 'You let the ice queen get you? Next time, go to the spot to the right of the drama stage. No one goes there. None of the teachers even know it exists!'

Grinning, I squeeze past him. 'Thanks! You can have this spot.'

Chapter Sixteen

Wednesday

Funmi, Alfie and I make a right down the blue corridor to get to Mr Sanders's class. While Alfie and Funmi are talking about science, we pass another talent show poster and I remember what BendItLikeC said about talking to friends.

I want to tell my friends about the support group, but I'm not ready.

'I signed up for the talent show auditions,' I blurt out instead.

Funmi squeals, gripping on my arm, and then hugs me. 'Yes! OMG, Sadé. We can practise together now.'

'That's ace! Sadé, Sadé, Sadé,' Alfie cheers. 'She shoots. She scores!'

Other people look at us and I can't stop a big smile from appearing on my face, but the smile drops after spotting Trina in the line.

Trina cuts her eyes at me but doesn't say anything.

'I can't believe Teni spoke to Trina earlier about what

happened in science,' Funmi whispers. 'When Teni said it was an accident and she should leave you alone, I'll never forget the look on Trina's face.'

Alfie sniggers on the other side of me. 'Yeah, she won't be saying anything bad to you again.'

The top of Mr Andrews's head peeks up above the rest of the students in the corridor. His eyes connect with mine, and he beckons me over.

My form class whisper behind my back as I walk slowly towards Mr Andrews. I'm half waiting for the beasts to appear.

'Hi, Sadé,' Mr Andrews says. 'I've been meaning to grab you for a quick chat, but I've been off work. It's about what happened in our last lesson with the cans.'

I look down at the new scuff mark on my black shoe.

'I'm sorry, Sadé.' He puts his hands on his chest. 'I know you would never have done anything like that on purpose. I shouldn't have left you unsupervised to handle that task alone. I take full responsibility. I'm really looking forward to your presentation next lesson . . . Oh, I think your class is going in, so I'll leave you to it.'

Whistling, Mr Andrews walks off down the corridor and I don't move until Mr Sanders clears his throat behind me.

'Sadé, we're waiting for you.'

Mr Sanders has a dark look of disapproval on his face, which matches perfectly with his black sweater vest.

'Sorry, sir.'

I shuffle inside and the door of doom closes behind me. For the whole of the maths lesson, I can't concentrate. *Mr Andrews thinks the cans were his fault, but it wasn't. It's those beasts. But how do I tell him that? My beasts are ruining my world and now this one, causing chaos wherever they go.*

There must be a solution. Maybe if I can trap them back inside my world, then I can handle them easier . . .

Mr Sanders moves through the desks, sliding our marked quizzes in front of us. 'I can definitely see improvements, but some of you still need to study harder.'

Mr Sanders places my paper on the desk. Turning it over, a red circle with 55% in stares back at me. My shoulders sag.

'Yes, I knew you could do it. That's a decent grade,' Alfie says, leaning closer to my desk and checking my paper. 'What's up, Sadé?'

Why isn't it higher?

The butterflies flutter at the corner of my eyes, crawling over my test. I thought I was getting better.

I take a deep breath in like Ellie said I should, but I choke on the burnt sweet and salt popcorn smell.

'Deep breath in, Sadé.'

The butterflies swarm around me, until I can't see anything but the mark.

'Deep breath in, Sadé, and imagine one of your favourite places.'

The butterflies crawl along my skin. I try to focus on my breathing, touching the locket Grandma gave me as I imagine myself at Hope Garden Centre with the sweet-smelling plants and the calming teas. I picture Mum there with me, laughing as she's telling stories.

'That's it, Sadé, well done.'

I don't know how long Alfie was waiting for an answer, but the words finally leave my mouth. 'I'm fine.'

At the end of class, Mr Sanders claps his hands to get our attention. 'Pack away quietly if you want to get out for lunch in this century.'

'Are we going to go to the field for lunch?' Funmi asks as she zips her bag up. 'I want to show you the new part we added to the dance.'

Alfie removes the football from his bag and shoves it

under his armpit. 'Yeah, and I can kick the ball about with Callum.'

As I'm about to respond, Mr Sanders interrupts. 'Can you both excuse us? I would like to speak with Sadé for a moment, please?'

Alfie dribbles the ball. 'We'll wait for you outside.'

'If you don't want me to confiscate that ball, Alfie, I suggest you hold on to it until you're at the field.'

When Mr Sanders's back is turned, Alfie mimics him before closing the door behind them.

With his crossed arms and a squinting smile, Mr Sanders asks, 'Can I see your test paper?'

I nod, rummaging through my bag for the test and hand it over to him. Mr Sanders looks down at it and then back at me.

'Have you been attending the Learning Lab? Has the extra support been helping?'

'Yes, sir.'

Mr Sanders hands the test paper back to me with raised eyebrows. 'Good. I'm trusting that you'll continue to apply yourself because there's still room for improvement.'

'Yes, sir.'

Mr Sanders isn't looking at me any more. His red pen moves quickly across the paper in front of him, destroying someone else's day.

'I believe there's a Learning Lab session now. I'd suggest you run along to that. You're dismissed.'

Will I ever be good enough?

I remember Mum's face. The sickness cut the fun. My grades finished what the illness hadn't done.

I rush outside the room, where Funmi and Alfie are waiting. They're talking, but they stop once they see me. My bag and crumpled test paper hit the floor. My heart races. I squeeze my eyes shut and lean against the wall. I try to imagine I'm back in Ellie's messy room.

'What's wrong, Sadé?' Funmi asks, putting her arm around me.

'Place one hand on your stomach just below your ribs and the other hand on your chest. Yes, perfect. Just like that. Now, you're going to inhale for four seconds and hold it in for another four seconds and then exhale for six seconds. Can you try that for me?'

My chest rises *1 . . . 2 . . . 3 . . . 4*

'Deep breath in, Sadé, and imagine one of your favourite places.'

I hold it in, imagining I'm surrounded by colour *1 . . . 2 . . . 3 . . . 4*

And let it all go like a balloon *1 . . . 2 . . . 3 . . . 4*

I swipe the tears off my face but they keep pouring. 'Nothing.'

Alfie is used to tears with Levi. 'Sadé, don't cry. What did Mr Boring say? Is it about your grades?'

'What about her grades?' Funmi asks, confused. Before I can snatch it away from her, Funmi picks up my quiz.

'Give it back,' I crack. 'Just leave me *alone*!'

'Sadé!' my friends shout as I run away.

I find myself outside the Learning Lab room even though I don't want to be here. I wipe my face and blow my nose with the tissue inside my blazer pocket.

'Yo, newbie.' Sunny waves from inside; the door is slightly ajar. I can see his skinny arms waving around like he's signalling for help. If Grandma saw him, she'd want to stuff him with Nigerian beans – they make you strong. Sunny grins as I approach the table, pushing his comic book away.

I drop my bag and pull out the chair without saying anything.

'Hmm. Did Mr Sanders say something to you?' Sunny asks.

'Yeah,' I grumble. 'He says *there's still room for improvement.*'

Sunny raises his eyebrow. 'Don't sweat it. In Year Seven, I got twenty per cent on one test because I was up watching *One Piece* and didn't sleep the night before.'

'A piece of what?'

Sunny laughs. '*One. Piece*. It's an anime TV series. It's got a character in it called Monkey D. Luffy, who wants to be king of the pirates. Anyways Mr Sanders called my dad saying he was "worried" about me and that I needed to apply myself. My parents took away everything I owned for a *whole* month! I was struggling like Luke Skywalker on Dagobah.'

I blink at him. Most of that meant nothing to me. Sunny shakes his head at my confused face. 'In *The Empire Strikes Back*, Luke was trying to deal with studying the force and taking down the Empire and finding out the truth about his dad. He was going through a lot, basically.'

'Mr Sanders is like Darth,' I reply.

'Mr Sanders doesn't like kids, man,' Sunny says. 'How'd your test go?'

I slide the creased piece of paper across the table. Sunny skim-reads it and turns it over.

'This is a good grade. Well done, newbie.'

'But – but I didn't get one hundred per cent. Can't you see what I got?' I ask, pointing at the red score.

Sunny wiggles his dark eyebrows. 'Was YouTube built in a day? No, it took time. Your test shows me that you're applying the techniques we went over. What did you get on the last quiz before this one?'

'I got thirty per cent.'

Sunny does a jerky dance move like a robot. 'Newbie, don't you know that's an increase of twenty-five per cent?'

Oh yeah! 'I didn't think about it like that.'

'Yup!' He pops the p. 'And it's OK if you don't like maths. I'm going to tell you a secret.' Sunny leans in closer and whispers, 'I don't like maths either.'

'But how can you not like maths when you're so good at it?' I ask, confused.

'Not so loud. My mum might be hiding in here.' He laughs. 'Maths is OK and I'm pretty decent at it, but I'm not in love with it or anything and I'm *definitely* not whipping out a calculator every second. Besides, it's all right not to love everything – or even be good at everything. You don't see me joining the rugby team. They'd snap me like a twig. You just need to find your thing.'

I think for a moment and say, 'I love writing poetry and I signed up for the talent show auditions.'

'See.' He dusts his hands together. 'I knew it. I bet poetry is *your* thing.'

I find myself grinning. Maybe Sunny is right. Maybe poetry *is* my thing.

Chapter Seventeen

After school

'*Girls in Transit* is starting, Sadé,' Tolani says, stretching forward on the sofa to reach the glass of apple juice on the table. 'I even got your popcorn. Come and watch.'

I pause in the hallway and grip the straps of my rucksack, eyeing the staircase. 'Sorry, I have lots of homework to do.'

I want to go into my world to see if Mum is there. I haven't seen her there in a while and I'm worried. I need to talk to her about today, especially about what Sunny said. Could poetry really be *my* thing? Words used to be *our* thing. And I need to check to see what else those beasts have done.

Teni fiddles with her gold hoops, narrowing her eyes. 'Is that girl still bothering you? Do I need to talk to her again?'

'No!' Clearing my throat, I try again. 'I mean . . . no, thanks. She hasn't said anything to me. It's . . . just . . . I have homework.'

Tolani stops chewing and watches me too. I feel like I'm under a microscope as they examine me.

Before either of them can say anything else, I hurry up the staircase to my room.

Closing the bedroom door behind me, I squeeze my eyes shut and enter my world.

* * *

I'd hoped that Mum would be waiting for me at the cliff this time because I need her, but she isn't.

The plant fist at the edge of the cliff remains clenched, so it can't cradle me like it normally would.

The auditions are in two days. I don't know if I can do it.

I sit down beside the fist with my legs crossed and look out over my world. It's exactly how I left it – still fairly faded, but with a pop of colour reaching the edges. Sitting in the silence, a single bird chirps, fluttering its white daffodil and red geranium wings.

'Mum,' I whisper to the air. 'Sunny says I need to find my thing. Writing and words was *our* thing. Do you think it can be mine now?'

The tears build up at the back of my eyes. If Mum's not here to tell me I can do it, then I'm not sure I can after all.

An idea flashes into my head – Mum's not here any more. But I know where she will be.

* * *

My eyes pop open back in the real world. I sprint down the stairs.

'I'm going to Funmi's to do homework!' I shout at my sisters as I rush to the door, with the laces on my white trainers undone.

The front door slams shut behind me and I message my friends.

ZOMBIE SLAYERS! (AND FUNMI)

Me: sorry I shouted earlier

please meet me outside Dulwich cemetery

it's important

The bus drops me outside. This is where Mum lives now. Shielding themselves from the light drizzle outside the cemetery's gates, Funmi and Alfie huddle in their coats.

Using my shoes to kick some dirt on the ground, I walk closer to them. 'I'm *really* sorry about before. I just didn't want anyone to see my mark.'

My shame is a hard stain of tomato stew on a white top that will never come off, embedded and permanent.

A glimpse of a smile crosses Funmi's lips as she meets my eyes. 'You still owe me a BBQ wing.'

We hug. Funmi never stays mad at me for too long.

'Don't worry about it, Sadé,' Alfie says, shaking out his wet hair. 'Are we here to see your mum? Maybe being here will make you feel better.'

'Yeah, I think it will.' *I don't have any other choice.*

I step on to the stony path, Alfie and Funmi follow behind. We've only been here once before and after fifteen minutes of walking, we're completely lost.

'I think I recognise this one,' Alfie says, pointing at a random grave.

'This place is starting to scare me.' Funmi shivers. 'There's no one else here.'

Something colourful catches my eye. I look up at the dense leaves of the cedar trees. Shooting down from the sky is Nix. She flies to my level, circles me and then takes off between the trees.

My friends walk on ahead, but I follow Nix in the opposite direction. *What is she doing here?*

I leave my friends behind and chase after her spear-shaped tail with its fiery tips. Dodging trees and gravestones,

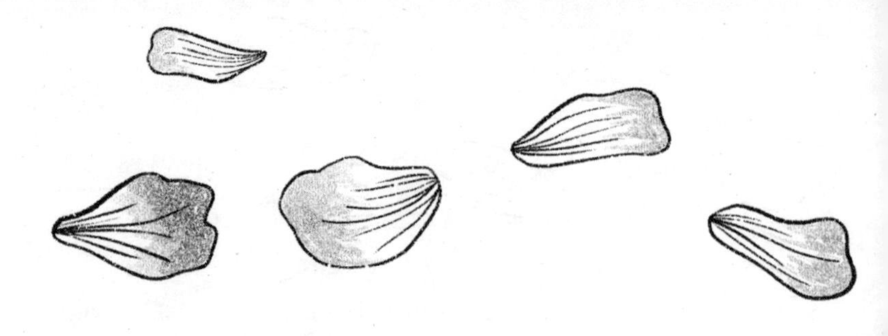

I stumble as twigs snap sharply under my trainers. Running deeper and deeper into the cemetery, I realise – Nix is taking me to Mum!

As the pathways get smaller, I remember back to that day. Our shiny black shoes hitting the grainy mud as we walked from the church to the patch of ground where Mum would now live. Rows of stone and the eleven gardenias along the way.

I count ten white gardenias now, then I spot the last blue gardenia rustling in the breeze.

Nix has disappeared, but she led me to Mum.

There are fresh sunflowers next to the wooden cross by her grave. Mum's favourites. Only Dad would bring her those, but it can't have been him. He said he wouldn't visit her grave.

I kneel by the wooden cross and close my eyes. Burying my head in my hands, I say, 'Mum, are you there?'

Nothing.

Why isn't Mum here? She's always here when I need her. Did something else bad happen?

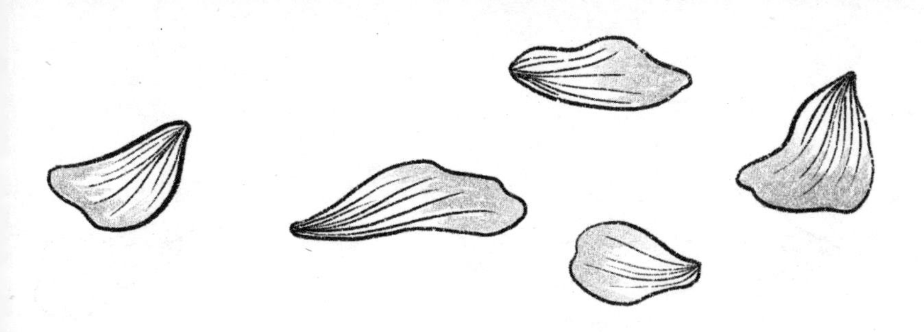

A branch snaps behind me. My back goes as stiff as an ironing board.

'Mum? Is that you?'

I look around, and a pair of red bloodshot snake eyes appear from behind the tree. With her protruding black claws dripping, Tiger draws her face back into a snarl, revealing her sharp canines.

'No,' I whisper. 'Not here.'

Then Hen hobbles forward, with her sharp marigold claws clinging to the soil. The cracked feathers look like they're about to shatter into a million pieces. Her eyes are unblinking.

There's a deep chuckle and a dark paw appears next. Fox strolls out. As if it can't get any worse, an enormous, eerie, inky version of Lion appears, surrounded by a sapphire mist. Lion's eyes flicker like Dad's indicators when he's turning right. There are surely too many spiked teeth to fit in his mouth.

A rumble turns into a loud roar, which hits me like a sonic wave, lifting me off the ground. My back hits the floor. Lion's jaws open so wide that I think his head is going to snap off.

'Leave me alone!' I shout at them. 'I liked how you were before!'

The beasts stamp.

Lion croaks as if he has a sore throat, 'It's too late. This is who we are now.'

'Deep breaths, Sadé. When you're feeling anxious, imagine one of your favourite places.'

The beasts surround me. All I can hear is my own raspy breathing, but I force myself to take in deep breaths, allowing the air to fill my lungs, opening them up. I imagine my world as it was before, with the chirping sounds, the sweet smells, and warm wind.

From somewhere, I find the courage to shout, 'Mum. People might say you're a memory or an echo! Something hollow, so low into a black hole that I can't go. They don't know that you're reality and this world is the memory. I wish I could get out of here and be free. If I could, I would spread my wings wide, hold on tight as we drift like smoke into the night, but it's not real. It's all "tell us how you feel, Sadé" and "you need to find a way to deal, Sadé". This isn't cards or a game of blackjack. I would swallow all the words I said, but it doesn't work like that.'

The beasts melt into the tree trunks, and I scramble up from the ground. There's a loud squawk as Nix reappears, circling the air above me.

'Sadé!' Tolani's voice shouts from somewhere.

Am I dreaming?

'Sadé!' she shouts again. 'Where are you?'

My head feels foggy.

Nix shoots off towards Tolani's voice and I stumble after, tracking her fiery tail. We pass rows of gravestones even more scary in the dark, as if the people are coming back to life. Then I see her. Through the trees, Tolani rushes towards me and she hugs me tightly, wrapping me in her warm coat. I feel like I can breathe properly again.

'Thank God Funmi messaged me,' Tolly says.

Funmi steps forward with Alfie beside her. 'Sadé, you were gone for so long. We got scared . . . we didn't know what to do.'

That's when I see Dad. I meet his reddened eyes.

'Thank God you're safe.' Dad marches forward and takes my hand.

As we're leaving the cemetery, I see Tiger again. She slinks from tree to tree, following us out.

The journey home in the car is quiet. I'm sandwiched between my friends in the back and Tolani cranes her neck from the passenger seat every few minutes to check if I'm OK. Every time I think Tiger's disappeared, I see her tail curling around the traffic lights we pass and her red eyes shining in between the streetlamps.

When we get home, I make sure that the door is locked so that Tiger doesn't come in after us.

Chapter Eighteen

'I'll make you some hot chocolate,' Tolani says as she shrugs off her black work coat. 'Do you still like it with marshmallows?'

We've dropped Alfie and Funmi at their houses and now it's just us. I nod and shuffle after Dad into the living room. With a heavy sigh, Dad lowers himself into the recliner chair and rubs at his eyes. I don't know where Teni is.

We sit in silence until Tolly comes back with the drinks.

'I made you coffee, Dad,' Tolani says, placing a tray full of steaming mugs on the coffee table. 'Here's your hot chocolate, Sadé.'

Dad's voice is quiet, but I can hear the anger in it. 'Why would you go to that place when I told you not to?'

'Dad, why don't you let her speak?' Tolani asks.

Footsteps race down the stairs and Teni appears in her school uniform, frowning. 'Sadé, why didn't you answer your phone? Do you know how many times we called you?'

My stomach bubbles.

Tolani stands by me, putting her hand on my shoulder. 'Let's not gang up on her. She just wanted to go and see Mum, right, Sadé?'

'Yeah,' I whisper, looking down at my hands.

Shaking his head, Dad replies. 'She's too young. It's as simple as that.'

I hold on to the locket, wishing Grandma was back here with me. If I pray hard enough, maybe she will come back.

'She isn't too young,' Tolani fires back. 'Mum is gone. It's important to grieve.'

'Tolly is right,' Teni agrees. 'I know Shadz shouldn't have just gone off like that, but why can't she see Mum?'

Dad hunches over in his chair, resting his elbows on his knees. We wait. After a few seconds of silence, he asks me, 'Are you hungry? It's almost time for dinner.'

It's not what I'm expecting. 'I . . . erm. Yes, I'm a bit hungry.'

We watch Dad go into the kitchen and look at each other, confused. Normally when Dad is upset about something, it takes him *ages* to calm down. He can't be *that* mad at me if he's making food.

Once the food is ready, Dad calls us to the table so we can eat. I take a big spoonful and chew. Rice and stew, sweet and comforting. I swallow and catch Dad looking at me.

'I'm sorry, Sadé.' Dad removes his round glasses and sets them on the table. 'Your sisters are right. I can't keep you from your mum. It's not right.'

I mix the grains of rice around in my plate. 'Thanks, Dad.'

'Eat, please. I don't want your food to get cold.'

My phone pings.

ZOMBIE SLAYERS! (AND FUNMI)

Funmi: it's Alfie's fault

he needed the toilet so we had to call your sister

Alfie: don't blame me

u were cold

u said we should call Tolani not me

Me: it's all right

I wanted to talk to mum
about the auditions
they're in two days

nothing is the same

Sadé is typing . . .

Tolani signed me up for this
grief support chat at school

it's helping me

Alfie: the woman with the pink
hair?

Me: Ellie

Funmi: that's cool

we can help you too 🙂

Alfie sends a photo of Pan smiling.

Alfie: hey

we beat 50 zombies with 2 paintballs

we can do anything

Chapter Nineteen

Thursday

Mr Andrews jiggles his keys outside the science room. 'Sorry, sorry! I got held up by my last class. Everyone inside. Alfie, Funmi and Sadé, go get set up. I can't wait to see what you've planned.'

We've practised the presentation over and over, till we memorised everything and it was perfect – but that doesn't stop my chest from quivering. *It has to go well.*

With his back to the rest of the class, Alfie holds out his fist to me and says, 'Ours is gonna be the best, Sadé.'

'And your audition tomorrow will be the best too,' Funmi adds.

'The best,' I reply with a smile.

I pound the bottom of my fist against the top of Alfie's and he does the same to me before we bump fists and swivel them around, rotating our wrists. I laugh. We haven't done our secret greeting since primary school. He does the same to Funmi. *I'm happy this isn't too uncool for her.*

Mr Andrews gives us the thumbs-up and moves off to the side with his notebook. As Alfie starts off our presentation, Fox pops up at the back of the classroom with a smirk on his face.

Alfie taps on the keyboard and our first slide appears. He flicks out a long stick pointer and bows. 'Welcome!' Alfie points the stick at Trina and Jas. 'We're gonna show you what a *real* presentation looks like.'

'Oooooh.'

'Yes, Alfie!' Callum shouts.

'Alfieeee,' Mr Andrews warns.

Clearing her throat, Funmi takes over, projecting her words exactly as we'd practised. 'We're going to be talking about chemical reactions – and to demonstrate them, we will be using the *very* popular elephant's toothpaste experiment . . .'

I find my mind wandering as she talks. My eyes scan the room. I think Fox has gone, but then he pops up again, peering around a desk, smiling.

'. . . Sadé will now speak about the aims of the experiment,' Funmi finishes.

This is it.

As I step forward, Fox steps forward too and my legs wobble. He grins playfully and his eyes glow.

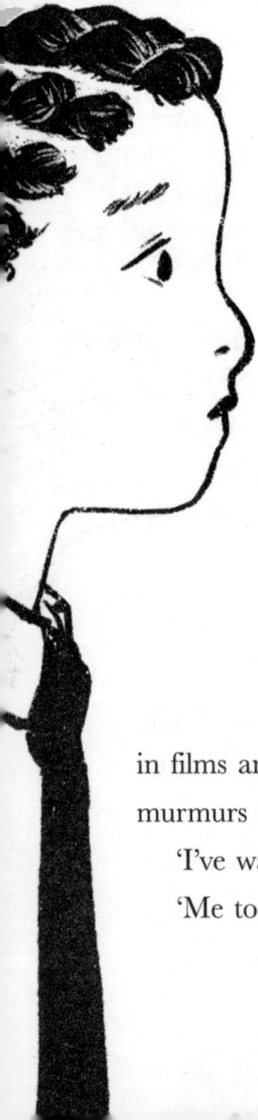

'Thank you,' I manage. 'In this experiment, we're going to . . . we're . . . going . . .' I stutter.

My palms sweat. I can do this. Jas gives me an encouraging smile.

Taking in a big breath, I try again and imagine myself in my world as it was, before things went wrong. I feel a warm breeze and breathe in fresh flowers. I open my eyes again and smile. Fox frowns.

'First,' I say, my voice smooth and confident, 'I'm going to discuss the experiment. This experiment creates a reaction called an *exothermic reaction.*' I pause. Fox takes a step forward, but he is uncertain. 'You may be thinking: what's an exothermic reaction?' Nodding at Alfie to change the slide, I point at the screen. 'Here is one example.'

I switch off the lights. The science room glows with short clips of cars exploding in films and rockets shooting off into the sky. I can hear murmurs of interest from the class.

'I've watched that film.'

'Me too!'

Alfie moves on to the next slide.

'So, an exothermic reaction is a chemical reaction where the substances reacting release energy as heat.' I flip back on the lights. Fox is still there, but he looks confused. 'Can anyone tell me what they saw in the clips?' I ask.

My classmates bounce up and down, hands in the air, trying to get me to pick them.

'Simone.'

'Burning?' she replies.

'Correct! One example of an exothermic reaction is burning, but in the experiment, foam . . .'

The more words I say, the more Fox's smile droops. He takes a step back and then another. And then, just as I am explaining the final point, he staggers and vanishes.

Alfie clicks on the last slide. I smile. 'Thanks for listening to our presentation.'

Alfie bows dramatically and everyone claps, including Mr Andrews, whose smile matches mine. My body settles in the chair, but my heart doesn't.

We did it.

Mr Andrews stands in the centre of the room. 'Well!

Talk about going out on a high. Thank you for all the presentations. I will give you your grades next lesson. Now it's time for the experiment. Can everyone get their lab coats and goggles on, please? All the equipment is on the tray in front of you and the instructions are there too. I will be coming round to help. You can start – Callum! Keep your goggles on. You're handling acid.'

Callum pretends to throw some on Alfie. 'Will it burn all his skin off, sir?'

Mr Andrews snatches the beaker from his hand. 'That's it. No experiment for you. Wait outside, please.'

'Yes, sir,' Callum sulks.

Picking up the laminated sheet, I read the instructions out. As Funmi leans on the table to grab the beakers, the table wobbles. Funmi kneels down to twist the table's uneven leg, but it shakes even more, causing the beakers to slide towards each other. I steady them with my hands.

'I'm trying to twist this thing,' she groans. 'It's not moving.'

Fox pops up at the edge of the table beside the beakers.

'Wouldn't it be funny if an *accident* was to happen?' Fox grins.

I move the beakers away from Fox and from Funmi. *I won't let him hurt my best friend.* Fox's beady eyes watches Funmi moving around under the table.

There's an evil gleam in his orange orbs. As the table shakes, everything moves in slow motion. Funmi's head pops back up from under the table and Fox's large paw swipes at the beaker of acid.

Quickly, I throw my body against the table, pushing Funmi out of the way and catching the beaker right before it crashes to the ground next to her.

'Oh my gosh, Sadé. You've got acid on your hand.'

Chapter Twenty

Nurse Coleen's office is full of 'hmms' and 'ahhs' as I tell her everything – apart from Fox, because he is my fault. The water from the cold tap freezes my hand.

Nurse Coleen eventually shuts off the tap. Gliding across the room on her chair, she gets an accident form to fill in and a tube of cream for me.

'Let me see,' Nurse Coleen says, examining my hand. 'Any pain or numbness?'

I shake my head. 'No.'

'Good.' Nurse Coleen squirts some of the white cream on to her gloved finger and gently rubs the cream in. 'Luckily, it was only a small amount of acid and the lowest concentration. I want you to monitor your hand. If you notice any redness, irritation or pus, then your parent or guardian needs to take you to see a doctor immediately.'

'Thanks, Nurse Coleen.'

I touch the spot on the back of my hand where the

acid fell and think about what happened. The presentation was going so well. It was as if the more I said, the weaker Fox became. But then he came back to ruin everything.

A line for a new poem comes to my mind. *Am I ready for the chill of change?*

As soon as I close Nurse Coleen's door, I run into Teni. When she left this morning, her braids were packed in the usual bun, but now her hair is down, and it looks messy. Like last night, there's a worried expression on Teni's face.

'Is your hand all right?' she asks, fiddling with the black headband wrapped around her wrist.

'How did you know I hurt my hand?'

Teni picks up my hand. Her shoulders sag as she sees the reddened skin. 'Funmi messaged me.'

Ellie's pink fringe appears from her 'tell me how you're feeling' office door.

'Sadé, you're right on time for our appoint—'

Shaking my head at her, I open my eyes wide, praying she gets it. Teni looks Ellie up and down.

'Never mind! My mistake!' she chirps, closing the door.

Teni squeezes her face. 'How comes that counsellor woman knows you?'

I run through excuses in my head, but Teni's raised eyebrows tells me she won't believe any of them.

'I'm in this anonymous grief support group.' The words are so quiet that I hope she doesn't hear.

Teni kisses her teeth. 'I *know* that Tolani must have signed you up for it. Don't lie.'

I don't say anything.

'Why do you need the group?' she asks. 'You've got me.' I don't say anything. Teni looks like she has something in her eye. She swallows. 'Anyways, I'm late for class. I'll see you later.'

She walks away, leaving me standing there.

As soon as I open the front door that afternoon, I see my sisters standing face to face in the centre of the living room. I want to turn around and leave again.

'Tell her, Sadé,' Tolani demands. 'Tell her that the support group is helping you.'

I sit down on the sofa. Before I can say anything, Tolani is talking again. 'The support group *and* the counsellor are helping her. It's something all of us in this house needs.'

'Whatever! She's not like you,' Teni replies, shaking her head. 'Not everyone wants to be you. I know that's why you didn't tell me. She's going around telling people our business.'

'The group is anonymous,' I say quietly.

Tolani talks over me. 'The group is anonymous! You don't *think* I thought of that? I'm in university, you know.'

Teni's phone rings loudly, adding more noise, but she silences it and throws it on to the sofa. Teni never usually ignores her phone. 'Whatever, man. You forged Dad's signature. I'm gonna tell him.'

Tolani laughs, but it doesn't sound like a happy one. 'Fine. I'll tell him you've been sneaking out and coming home late.'

I thought I was the only one who hears Teni leave in the night. Teni looks surprised and her eyes find mine, but I never told.

Tolani storms into the kitchen with Teni right behind her and I follow, worried they're going to keep on fighting. Tolani pulls open the fridge door and slams down ingredients for lasagne on to the counter. 'What? You think I didn't know?' she asks. 'This family needs to stop running away from problems! We haven't even spoken about going to church since Grandma left. Why? Because we don't want to upset Dad. Sadé got hurt today and I bet we won't talk about that either.'

'I'm not running from nothing, all right,' Teni replies, and her voice simmers down like a pot of stew on low heat. 'I just go for walks to clear my head when I'm thinking about Mum.'

I stare at her. I hadn't realised Teni needed time to herself. She always seems so calm and unbothered.

Tolani stops slamming food on the counter and turns to Teni.

They're fighting because of me.

It's all my fault again.

Replace negative thoughts with proactive ones.

'The group helps me,' I say. 'We talk about things that help us when we're angry or upset. Talking to the group – and Ellie – makes me feel better.'

'Really?' Teni asks.

'Yeah, she's nice. I've been writing more again.' I smile, thinking about how full my journal is getting. 'And I signed up for the talent show. The auditions are tomorrow.'

'You what?' Tolani exclaims. 'See, I told you it was going to help.' She comes over and pulls me into a tight hug.

'Calm down, man.' Teni's words are muffled. 'She can't even breathe.'

Tolly releases me and looks down at me, a proud look on her face. Leaving the kitchen, we all sit on the sofa with Teni sitting opposite me. 'You better not embarrass me at the auditions. I have a reputation.'

Tolani's teal, patterned cushion hits Teni right in the forehead. 'What reputation?'

'Why did you hit me?' Teni yells, swinging her cushion to connect with Tolani's body.

She catches me laughing. 'Oh, so you think this is funny, yeah?'

My sisters share a glance before they both turn on me with their cushions. I sprint out of the living room as they chase me laughing and screaming. We beat each other with cushions until we're out of breath and tuck into the lasagne once it's ready.

Later on in the evening, there is a knock at my bedroom door and Dad walks in. He shifts around, trying to find a comfortable position on the edge of my bed.

'Your teacher called,' Dad says. 'How is your hand?'

Dropping my eyes, I touch the spot with my fingertips. 'It's better now. The nurse told me to keep an eye on it for . . .' I hesitate, struggling to remember what the nurse told me.

'Redness, irritation and pus,' he finishes, and reaches out to check my hand. 'I've been letting you down and I haven't been listening to you. It shouldn't be like this. I know I don't have an excuse, but without your mum . . .'

'It feels like something is missing,' I finish.

Dad makes a funny sound. 'Yes, it does.' He grips my foot and shakes it about like he used to, making me giggle. 'I can't replace your mum, but I can try to be better . . . for you girls.'

Ellie says trying is good enough. The large lump in my throat and the burning behind my eyes stop me from talking so I nod instead.

Dad leaves and I snuggle deep into my duvet, enjoying the silence as Teni hasn't come upstairs yet. Dad's words pivot in my mind.

ZOMBIE SLAYERS! (AND FUNMI)

Me: my hand is better

Funmi:

Alfie: have you got super-powers now

I put my phone down. Usually, Mum would tell me a story if I couldn't sleep, but she's not here, so instead I turn on my glowing bird lamp and pick up my journal. I start a new poem with the line that's been stuck in my head all day.

Am I ready for the chill of change?

I close my eyes and enter my world.

* * *

The crowd-surfing grass lifts me up on to my back so I'm gazing up at the sky. The spiky edges of the grass become smooth before my eyes like they were before. Sitting up, my pen hits the page once again as the poem forms.

Seasons

Am I ready for the chill of change?
Biting, bruising change,
Warmth in the normal,
Warmth in staying the same,
What if I let the chill in?
Knitted scarf undone,
Goosebumped skin.
Does remembering mean I
want the warmth of the past to fade?
Does remembering mean
I'm not ready for the chill
of change?

Am I ready?

Looking out over my world, the colour flickers again, bleeding brighter from one end to the other, but the colour still doesn't quite reach the edges like before. When will the full colour come back? Gone is the burnt smell that polluted the air, and now a whiff of freshly popped sweet and salt popcorn travels past my nose, making me hungry. Nix hovers in front of me, her squawks joining the other sounds that I thought I'd never hear again. The chirping, tweeting, buzzing and squealing echoes around my world as the creatures come alive. My world is *almost* back to normal, but those beasts are still out there.

* * *

I open my eyes and leave my journal spread out on the bed, feeling ready for the auditions tomorrow.

Chapter Twenty-One

Friday

It's the day of the auditions.

Standing backstage with Funmi, I pull out my purple journal and go over my poem again. Funmi and the twins have already auditioned. I feel like a balloon pumped with air, ready to burst.

A short white boy pokes his head through the curtain. Running his pencil down the clipboard, he pauses. 'Sadé, you're up next after the dance group on stage now. Break a leg.'

I *really* hope I don't.

We poke our heads through the curtain to see Trina prancing around on stage with Jas and Simone as her back-up dancers. They perform a synchronised slide across the stage and then do a scooped arm into a hip sway to the beat. They lift their chests and drop them back down so their bodies roll, and then they repeat it. They're really good! Jas's face is a crumpled crisp packet though. *I wonder why she's upset.*

Funmi moves closer to me, and her hair tickles the side of my face. 'I didn't know they'd be that good,' she whispers.

'Your trophy will be right next to Femi's. You know what their act doesn't have?'

Funmi looks at me expectantly. 'What?'

I channel my best Funmi. Standing with my hips out and my arms bent at an awkward angle, I reply, 'No seasoning at all.'

Funmi grins and hugs me. 'Why are your arms bent like that though? You look like a chicken, Sadé.'

We giggle until the music stops and the judges clap. Trina steps out from in front of the curtain. 'The judges *loved* us,' she boasts to Jas and Simone.

Trina's eyes flip to mine. Holding my breath, I wait for her to say something, but instead she marches off with Simone. Jas leaves through the other exit. *That's strange . . .*

The curtain is pulled back and the boy points at me.

'You're up.'

My feet carry me on to the stage, but my chest is still back there with Funmi. The only thing that could make this worse is if the beasts appeared. I haven't seen one of them since our science presentation, and my world is getting much better – but I know they're still out there. They're always creeping on me like shadows. *Sadé and her shadow beasts.*

'Welcome, Sadé. What will you be dazzling us with today?' Mr Lawrence asks.

Shuffling from foot to foot, I reply, 'A poem.'

Mr Lawrence smiles and gestures towards me. 'Per-fect. Please begin whenever you're ready.'

My arms hang at my sides as silence fills the hall. I look carefully around, but there are no beasts or butterflies. Funmi is sitting in the front row, and she gives me an encouraging smile.

1 . . . 2 . . . 3 . . . 4

You might not be able to see it, Fọlásadé, but you have the same fire within you.

1 . . . 2 . . . 3 . . . 4 . . . 5 . . . 6

You just need to find your thing.

I take another breath and hold on to the locket for extra courage.

'My poem is called "The Beasts Inside".' I begin.

'Your stories are part of me,
I store more of you inside of me,
See
your words photosynthesised –
breathed life . . .'

I carry on, lost in my words, until I reach the end and there is silence.

'Wonderful!' Mr Lawrence exclaims, getting up out of his seat and clapping. 'Thanks for that amazing poem, Sadé. A great piece. The results of the audition will be released at the beginning of next week.'

I run off the stage.

'Sadé, you were *so* good,' Funmi squeals, jumping up and down.

If I can do this, maybe I can face the beasts and Ellie.

I head to Ellie's office. The door squeaks open. I trudge into the room and my bag hits the side of the chair, ringing where the pins hit the metal leg.

'Hi, Sadé! I'm so sorry if I caused any problems between you and your sister yesterday.'

'It's all right,' I reply. I'm still buzzing from the audition.

'Phew, glad to hear it.' Ellie picks up her mug and takes a sip. 'Other than me messing things up, what else has been going on in Sadé's world?'

'Grandma left. And . . . I think Old Dad is coming back. I went to the cemetery to try and see Mum. but that didn't go the way I wanted it to. It was my fault. I've been writing in the journal you got me. I auditioned for the talent show, and it was great . . . and the science presentation was the best, but then there was the accident with the acid. I feel like it's all my fault.'

I thought it was supposed to get easier. It feels as though I have five angry horses galloping in my chest and I can't catch my breath. Gripping on to the chair, I try to focus on my breathing.

'Just like we practised, Sadé. Take a deep breath in.'

All the air rushes in like a hoover. *1 . . . 2 . . . 3 . . . 4.*

'Good. Now, hold it for four seconds.'

I count the coffee ring stains on Ellie's desk, which overlap like a Venn diagram.

'Almost there . . . and out for six seconds.'

1 . . . 2 . . . 3 . . . 4 . . . 5 . . . 6

I count the number of journals on Ellie's messy shelf, trapping the thoughts of people like me.

Ellie waits for a few minutes until I can speak again. 'Are you happy to continue?'

I nod.

Ellie tucks both of her feet under herself, so she's

sitting like a pretzel. 'Just now, you said, "It was my fault." You said it at least twice. In the last support group, we spoke about signs and symptoms of grief, and you put down . . .' She checks her notebook. '*Anxious, guilt, scared.* Those are some *big* feelings. Don't keep those big feelings trapped inside. It seems to me that your guilt could be wrapped in situations you can't control. Not everything is your fault.'

I don't say anything, but I nod. She smiles.

'I would love for you to think about what makes you feel better. Think about what works for you, Sadé. Deal?'

I nod.

'Great, and before we continue, I'm reminding everyone about the support group home task for next week. It would be good if you found something that represents your mum or a memory of her, and leave it at the drop box in reception – then we can discuss it in group.'

Take a deep breath in, Sadé.

When everyone is asleep, I creep out of my room. I push open Mum's study door and walk in. Mum's favourite mint chocolates are sitting open on the desk. About half are missing. Dad and Mum used to share the chocolates when they came home from work.

Bending down, I run my fingers over the familiar

patterns of Mum's special box and lift the lid up. My eyes dart over the animal puppets and fabric inside. Mum used the puppets to perform stories for the customers at Hope Garden Centre every last Saturday of the month. Mum's sessions were the most popular. I take one of the puppets out for the support group home task.

Tuesday

Grief Support Group Chat [4]

Ellie[moderator]: Hey everyone! I hope you've been well. Before we move on to the session for today, let's do a brief recap. Last week we looked at the signs and symptoms of grief, our grief cycles and briefly on how to deal with feelings. Has anyone used any of the techniques that we spoke about?

Anon05: yh

Ellie[moderator]: Great. Would you mind sharing with the group?

Anon05: ur worksheet thing said we can howl when we get angry but mr sanders sent me out

You'reDaObiWan4me: the worksheet said howl at the moon LOL what did you do?

Anon05: I howled during his maths lesson haha

I burst out laughing in the library and the librarian shushes me, but I can just imagine Mr Sanders's face. I wish I'd been there.

You'reDaObiWan4me: ahwooooooooo
BendItLikeC: did he turn into a werewolf LOOL
Anon05: yh with his red sweater vest HAHA
Ellie[moderator]: OK. Thanks for that @Anon05.

Today's session will be focused on memories and we're also going to be discussing some questions about personal grief. Does anyone have a special place that reminds you of your loved one?

BendItLikeC: tate gallery
Anon05: batting cages
OnceUponaTime: hope garden centre church

Tolly was right – we haven't been to church since Grandma left. Without Dad, it doesn't feel right. We don't want to upset him, but I do want to go.

Ellie[moderator]: Those are some wonderful places. When you are ready, you can go and visit – or you may have done so already. Visiting a place linked to your loved one can make you feel closer to them.

Will Hope Garden Centre be the same without Mum there? I can't imagine going and not hearing her say to me, 'Are you ready to feed your imagination, Sadé?'

Ellie[moderator]: For your home task, I asked you to leave something in the box at reception that represents your person/a good memory of them. I'm going to give everyone the opportunity to share more about the item they left in the box.

Ellie shared a picture

Ellie[moderator]: Please can you let the group know what you left in the box and share why it represents your loved one/a good memory.
BendItLikeC: I left one of tim's photographs from the lake district waterfall

I was bored

tim waited for 1 hour to get the perfect photo

I could see why he waited. The photo is epic

Ellie[moderator]: Thanks, @BendItLikeC. It is very epic indeed!

BendItLikeC: they're doing an exhibition for his pics this weeknd

at the park

I'm not going

You'reDaObiWan4me: why not?

BendItLikeC: because

Anon05: I thought he was ur best mate

BendItLikeC: he was

his mum didn't like me

don't think she wants me there

Anon05: I wud still go

You'reDaObiWan4me: they can't stop you from going in

BendItLikeC: they can't?

You'reDaObiWan4me: yeah

the park is a public space

Ellie[moderator]: If it's important to you, decide whether it's worth going. You can always take someone else along for support.

BendItLikeC: it's not only that

Tim is not there

what's the point?

I get it. Mum wasn't there at the cemetery, so what was the point? It's not the same – it won't ever be the same. It's like watching your favourite movie for the second time. You can't get the first tingles back.

OnceUponaTime: I went to see my mum's grave to talk

sometimes I still imagine mum is speaking to me

BendItLikeC: what was that like

It was like going to cinema and sitting down, but there's a big hole where the screen should be.

OnceUponaTime: sometimes

I see parts of her in other places

Like in the way my sisters look after me or in my own writing.

tim's thing could help you

a bit of him is there

BendItLikeC: maybe I will go

I didn't think of it like that

Ellie[moderator]: Thanks for contributing, group, and I hope you can come to a decision @BendItLikeC. Does anyone else want to share?

Anon05: @You'reDaObiWan4me did u leave the slipper

You'reDaObiWan4me: @Anon05 I thought you would've burnt the box

Anon05: haha thought about it after I saw the slipper

Ellie[moderator]: I'm glad nothing was burnt. Do you want to share more about the slipper @YoureDaObiWan4me?

You'reDaObiWan4me: my gma used to throw it when I annoyed her

that slipper was hard man

RIP

Anon05: LOL

Ellie[moderator]: Thanks. Anyone else?

OnceUponaTime: I left the fox puppet

BendItLikeC: @OnceUponaTime love the ears on your fox

Ellie[moderator]: Can you tell us a bit more about the fox @OnceUponaTime?

OnceUponaTime: fox is a character from one of mum's stories

he was always doing something sneaky and getting into trouble

You'reDaObiWan4me: sounds like @Anon05

Ellie[moderator]: Amazing, thanks for sharing that story.
@Anon05, you didn't leave an item in the box? Is there anything you can think of that represents your person?
Anon05: no
BendItLikeC: what about the batting cage thing you told me about
Ellie[moderator]: Would you like to share it with the rest of the group **@Anon05**?
Anon05: dad got me into baseball
we used to go to the batting cages together
You'reDaObiWan4me: I can't even swing a bat
Anon05: lol I could hit it far too
Ellie[moderator]: Thanks for sharing, @Anon05. It's great sometimes to share some good memories of our loved ones and I hope it helped you. Great. Now we're going to be looking at some discussion questions. I want everyone to pick one or two they don't mind talking about.
Ellie[moderator]: @OnceUponaTime and @You'reDaObiWan4me. You have chosen the same discussion point of 'How do other members of your family express their grief?'

You'reDaObiWan4me: my mum is always making us drink turmeric milk

BendItLikeC: why?

You'reDaObiWan4me: it's good for your immune system

she worries we'll get sick

and dad started cooking but it tastes like sweaty socks

Anon05: LOL hw do you know what ur dads socks tastes like

You'reDaObiWan4me: Ha long story

OnceUponaTime: @You'reDaObiWan4me my older sister worries about me too

Ellie[moderator]: It's very common for grief to make people worry more about how short life is and it can make people want to bring their families closer. Do you know anyone who has reacted in an opposite way?

OnceUponaTime: my dad

New Dad, that is. Could he slowly be changing into Old Dad again?

OnceUponaTime: he doesn't talk about mum a lot

Ellie[moderator]: People grieve in many different ways as I've been saying – one size does not fit all. Talking about someone a person has lost can be hard for some and easier for others.

Ellie[moderator]: And the last discussion point chosen was to finish off this sentence opener 'One of my biggest fears is . . .'

My phone vibrates with the answers from the group, but I can't focus on them. The sentence is stuck in my head because when I close my eyes, all I see are the beasts.

Ellie[moderator]: That's the end of the session for today and thanks for sharing.

How do you feel after this session?
What did you take away from this session?

Chapter Twenty-Two

Mr Sanders's clap at the front of the classroom snaps Funmi's head up. 'Miss Akindele. Your mouth hasn't stopped moving throughout this whole lesson. Should I sit down while you teach the lesson instead?' Pausing with the whiteboard pen in his hand, Mr Sanders glares. 'No? Then you can answer question 5. Calculate the distance.'

Funmi fumbles over the numbers because instead of listening, she's been whispering with the twins about when the audition results will be released.

'Anyone else?'

Looking at the textbook, I mumble the formula for working out distance that I went over with Sunny.

'Six miles,' I mutter.

Mr Sanders's head turns like a key and his eyes lock on to mine. 'What was that, Sadé? I can't hear you. Speak up.'

Numbers fly through my head, but I still get the same answer. 'Six miles. I th . . . The answer is six miles.'

I hold my breath as Mr Sanders hesitates for a second. His forehead goes as wrinkly as the brain Mr Andrews once showed us.

'Six miles is correct.'

I *actually* got it right.

'Way to stick it to Mr Boring, Sadé.' Alfie grins at me from his desk.

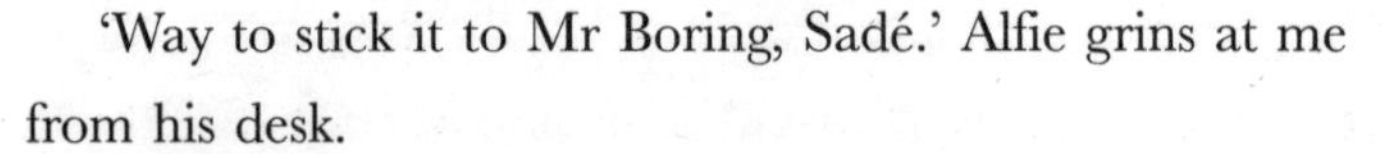

For the rest of the day I'm cruising
in my bubble sea
because, for once, I beat maths and it
didn't beat me.

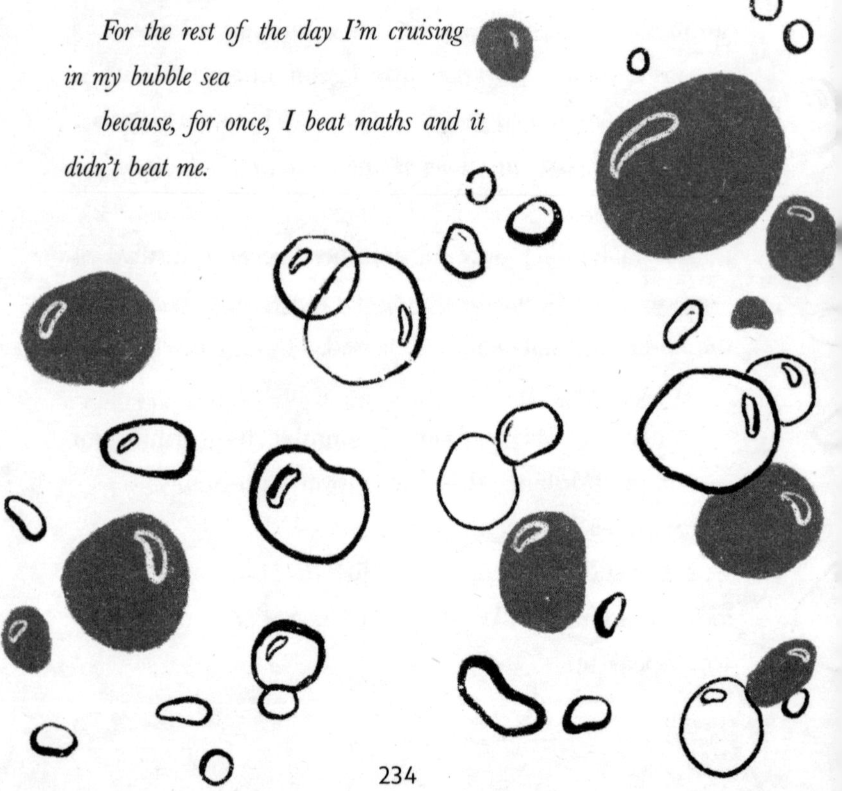

The look on Mr Sanders's face makes me forget my anxiety about the beasts and the audition results, until we get to PE.

Once we've all changed into our itchy PE kits, Miss Greenleaves makes us all stand in a line in the school hall. I fidget – the blacks shorts are riding up, giving me a wedgie.

Miss Greenleaves shoves some of her escaping frizzy blonde hair back under her white headband. 'We're playing netball today but first you need to warm up.' She jogs on the spot. 'You're going to run around the hall clockwise to get the blood flowing. Go, go, go!'

Alfie shoots off like a rocket with Callum. Sweat forms on my forehead. I jog past Jas, sitting on the bench with a bandage wrapped around her wrist.

'Did you hear what happened to her?' Funmi asks, slowing down to my pace. I know she's going to tell me anyway. 'I heard that she hurt her arm bungee jumping.'

Miss Greenleaves jogs past me with her knees almost up to her chin. 'I see some people are slowing down. Pick those knees up!'

Trina jogs in front of us. She's pointing and laughing at one of our classmates who tripped on their shoelaces. I bet she wouldn't be laughing if *she* fell down. As I use all my energy to pass her, I don't see the stray tennis ball on the floor and my legs tangle. I crumble to the floor. The *slap* as I land echoes across the hall. I hear the sniggers from Trina behind me.

With a burning face and a sore knee, I jump up, but Trina doesn't say anything as she passes by.

Miss Greenleaves bounces towards me. 'That was a nasty fall there. Maybe you should sit this one out.'

I nod. Blowing her whistle, she hollers at the rest of the class. 'One more lap! Go, go, go!'

My sides hurt and now my knee is sore. I limp over to the benches to sit next to Jas. While Alfie and Callum play-fight in front of me, Funmi tucks her head between her legs, breathing heavily, then runs over to the bench. 'You . . . you . . . all right?'

'Yeah,' I grumble, rubbing my knee.

Miss Greenleaves blows her whistle, waving Funmi back over. Jas and I watch as she throws netball bibs at the class. Miss blows her whistle again, and the game begins. Within a minute, there's pushing between Funmi and Trina.

'Off the court, both of you! Stand on opposite sides of the hall!'

Jas sniggers and I can't hold my laugh in. As Jas shifts on the bench, she flinches in pain and holds on to her bandaged wrist.

'Did you really go bungee jumping?' I ask, pointing to her injury.

'No, I was just bringing some stuff down from the loft with my mum and I bumped my wrist on the door,' she replies. 'Sadé. I've been wanting to talk to you for ages. I'm sorry about what I've done. I want us to go back to normal.'

My mouth hangs open and the blood roars in my ears as my breathing picks up speed like a train. 'You bullied me. You and Trina. And . . . and you let her say mean stuff about me.'

In church they say you can tell who someone is by their fruits. If Trina was a fruit, she would be the sour green apple at the bottom of the fruit bowl.

Jas slides closer to me. 'I'm *really* sorry. It's just that no one tells you what secondary school is like, and . . .' Jas looks down at her lap. 'I know it's not an excuse, but I wanted to fit in. I swear I didn't know Trina was like that before.

I know she's not a good person. Can we be friends again?'

Friends don't treat each other like Jas treated me. I know Jas wants to cry because she starts rubbing the top of her ear.

'No, you're not my friend. You can't be.'

I leave Jas sitting there, while I sneak into the changing room to grab my journal. All the feelings swirling around in my head, land on the page.

A braid,
We were once as
tight as,
You played
like it was all
a game.
Weighed
like my words.
My heart
was changed,
Left alone like a stray.

As the words keep pouring out on the page, the angry fog clears from my brain. I can finally take in a deep breath and go back outside.

'Great match, everyone!' Miss Greenleaves yells. 'I need some volunteers to help put everything back in the cupboard, including the equipment for the class outside.'

I raise my hand to volunteer. Jas does too when she sees mine. *Why is she doing this?* She can't even help because of her wrist.

'Are you sure, Jasmine?' Miss Greenleaves asks. 'What about your wrist?'

Jas nods eagerly. 'Yes, miss. I can use my other hand to pick up equipment. I want to help.'

'OK. If you're sure, then go ahead.' She beams at us, then frowns at Trina and Funmi. 'You two. Why don't you help them put all the equipment back into the cupboard?'

We work quickly and in silence. Soon everything is back inside the cupboard.

'Miss, can I go now?' Trina moans, walking towards Miss Greenleaves. 'I put most of the things away.'

Funmi's mouth flies open. 'No, miss. She's lying,' she replies, going after Trina.

The bulging equipment cupboard groans. It's stuffed to overflowing in there. Using all my strength, I slam my back against the door, but it's no use. Jas drops her bag and presses her back against the door too. The pressure from the cupboard propels us forward.

'Watch out!' I yell.

Balls, bats and badminton sets spring out in random directions as the door flies open. Jas throws herself on the

floor beside me with her hands covering her head. A volleyball thumps Miss Greenleaves on her right cheek. Trina dives on to the floor, narrowly missing the basketball, but Funmi is too slow. The ball smacks her in the stomach.

Whimpering, Funmi cradles her stomach and rocks from side to side. 'Owwww.'

'Funmi! Are you all right?' Miss Greenleaves helps Funmi up. 'That silly equipment cupboard. I've said a hundred times, we need more storage, but no one listens to me. I'm just glad you girls weren't hurt.'

Trina moans and dusts off her PE shorts. 'I can't believe this. I'm telling my dad. Endangered by school property.'

Miss Greenleaves looks concerned, pulling at her headband. 'Now, Trina, I don't think that's necessary. It was just an accident.'

Jas snorts. I catch her eye and we share a small smile. Then Jas turns to Trina. 'What would you tell your dad about? The ball didn't even touch you.'

Trina glares at Jas. 'You should be on *my* side – we're friends.'

Jas shakes her head and replies, 'Not any more. You can't be mean to everyone and expect them to stay mates.'

'Now, girls . . .' Miss Greenleaves starts.

'I don't need you anyways,' Trina spits, barging Jas with her shoulder, then pointing at me. 'And you're still a loser.'

While Trina storms towards the changing rooms, Jas leaves the sports hall.

As we make our way down the corridor to our next lesson, it's all Funmi can talk about. I can't believe Jas said that to Trina.

'Callum said that Jas punched Trina the other day and that's why her hand is all bandaged,' Alfie says excitedly.

Jas used to set spiders that she found in her house free. I remember the time when I helped her with the injured budgie in her back garden.

I shake my head. 'Jas wouldn't do that,' I reply. 'And

that's not what happened. Jas hurt her wrist helping her mum bring stuff down from the loft.'

Mrs Karoma unlocks her door as we arrive for English. As I pass her desk to go to mine at the back of the classroom, she whispers to me, with a huge smile on her face, 'Congratulations, Sadé. I *knew* you would make it through to the talent show.'

My feet stop moving.

'I – I made it?' I stutter. 'What?'

'Sadé!' Funmi squeals. 'We got in!'

Funmi shoves her phone in front of my face. I look down to see that someone has messaged Funmi a photo of the audition list and my name is there.

I gasp and cover my mouth in surprise. *This can't be real. I couldn't have got in.* But when I look at the phone again, the results remain the same.

'I got in,' I whisper.

Poetry is my thing.

'Yes!' Alfie shouts. 'You both got in!'

Alfie's blazer swings as he kicks his ball up and it lands on his head. The whole class cheers. He flicks it back down and does some twisting things with his feet.

'Thank you, Alfie,' Mrs Karoma laughs. 'Settle down. Books out, please, and phones away. What is it, Trina?'

'Can I switch seats?' she asks, cutting her eyes at Jas,

sitting beside her.

Mrs Karoma's smile flips like a switch. 'Trina. You know my rules about changing seats during the school term.'

Trina sulks, angling her body away from Jas as if she's infectious.

Mrs Karoma turns back to the board, and we're submerged in a Shakespeare stew for a whole hour, but I can't concentrate because I actually made it into the talent show. Me.

'Pack away, please,' Mrs Karoma says. 'Don't forget that your homework is due next lesson. No excuses, please.'

As we're packing away, upper-schoolers flock into the classroom, and Mrs Karoma changes her screen to the 'English Lit Club' slide.

Ashaunna's long, black and gold feed-in cornrows sway around her as she enters the room in her fitted black blazer, pleated skirt and knee-length black socks. She makes the uniform look cool.

Mrs Karoma finishes stacking some books. 'Ashaunna, I have someone for you to meet. Her name is Sadé.'

'I know Sadé,' Ashaunna says. 'You're Teni's little sister, right?'

Mrs Karoma winks at me. 'Well, Sadé is more than Teni's little sister. She's a talented young poet who got through the auditions for the talent show.'

Ashaunna's flowery perfume smells like a summer's day

in my world. 'Congrats for getting through. I heard the competition was really hard this year. You know, I'm a poet too.' A smile splits my face in two because she loves words like I do. 'Do you post your poems online?'

Shaking my head, I reply, 'Erm, no. But my work is in reception.'

Ashaunna clicks her fingers together. 'Wait, of course. I've read your poem.'

A tingling feeling works its way up my neck and across my face.

She read *my* poem.

'Really?'

'Yeah.' She points at me. *'Bullies destroy, uproot, their vines choking lives so we can't shoot.* I love that poem.'

'Told you Sadé was talented,' Mrs Karoma calls from the front, drawing attention from around the room, which makes my stomach flutter. Everyone is watching me.

I stare at the desk because I don't know where to look.

'I can help you, if you want, with the talent show,' Ashaunna offers, making me look up at her. 'We can practise together. What do you think?'

I grin widely. 'Yeah, I'd like that.'

'Here,' Ashaunna says, handing me her phone. 'Put your number in so I can message you later about practice.'

SISTERS

Me: I got into the talent show! 

Teni: I knew you wouldn't embarrass me

Tolly: I KNEW IT!! I told you.

Chapter Twenty-Three

Later on that day

'You got any food?' Alfie asks, peering over my shoulder as we wait outside Mr Andrews's room.

'What happened to all yours?' I ask.

Alfie slides his forehead against the locker beside us. 'The ice queen caught me selling the sweets and gave me two weeks' detention.'

Feeling sorry for Alfie, I dig through my bag for my pack of mini croissants. 'What about Hailey's birthday?'

He shrugs as he stuffs one in his mouth, the chocolate oozing out.

'Coach said I need to stop messing about. Says I could go far with football if I commit myself. All those detentions are boring anyways.'

'Did Mrs Williams take all your food?'

'Yes,' Alfie groans. 'The ice queen's probably frozen it by now.'

Mr Andrews appears at the front of the line with his

hands tucked in the pocket of his lab coat. 'Good afternoon, young scientists. Come in and get settled.'

Once we're seated, he gets our attention. 'I'll call each presentation group up one at a time, tell you your scores and give you a slip with some feedback.'

Mr Andrews unlocks his desk drawer to retrieve the gradebook. He only locks it because last year Callum tried to give everyone Us. The drawer must be jammed with papers because he pulls hard. It doesn't budge. He tries again and again, and his face gets red and sweaty.

'Sir, do you need some of my muscles?' Alfie asks, flexing his arms.

Mr Andrews scratches the top of his head. 'No, I'm good, Alfie, but thanks for offering.'

My hand flies up without me thinking.

'What is it, Sadé?' he asks.

I pull at a thread on my navy jumper. 'Sir, erm, you taught us about force and, uh, movement.'

Mr Andrews tugs some more at the drawer. 'What was that? Sorry, I just can't . . . seem to get this open.'

'I was just wondering – can you use a metal ruler as a lever, to generate force to open it?'

He stares at me, then clicks his fingers. 'That's brilliant, Sadé. Alfie, you can help by getting me a metal ruler.'

Alfie salutes Mr Andrews and gets him one from the

cupboard. Mr Andrews sticks the ruler in the gap and cranks it, until eventually the drawer pops open. He holds his notebook above his head with a smile. Alfie whoops. The whole class claps.

'Thank you. Trina and Jas. Can you come up first, please?'

The whispering around the room sounds like bees buzzing in my ear. Mr Andrews holds up his notebook to show them their grades and gives them a slip of paper each.

There's a knock at the door, but it's not just *any* knock. We all know who it is. As Mr Andrews fixes his tie, the whole class goes silent. Pulling open the door, Mrs Williams enters. Her heels tap against the floor. Her eagle eyes wander around the classroom to see if a shirt is scruffy, or that we're wearing the right shoes.

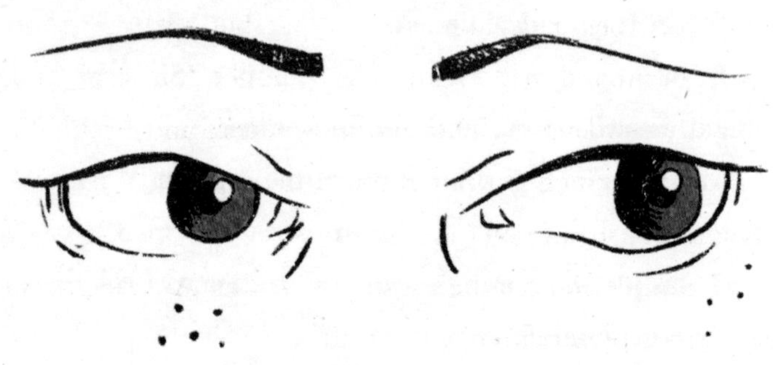

'Good afternoon, class,' Mrs Williams calls.

'Good afternoon, Mrs Williams,' we reply in unison, sitting up straight.

'Mr Andrews. Can I borrow you outside for a moment, please?' she asks. 'I won't keep you long.'

'I'll be back in a moment to give out the rest of the results,' Mr Andrews says to the class.

As soon as the door closes, Trina peers around, making sure we're all listening. 'Mr Andrews said *our* presentation was his favourite.'

Jas's mouth falls open. 'You're lying, Trina. Mr Andrews *never* said that.'

'I knew it,' Funmi mutters to me.

The door opens, and Mr Andrews comes back inside the room. 'Thanks for waiting, class. Where was I?' Mr Andrews clutches the slips in his hands. 'Alfie, Funmi and Sadé, come up, please.'

'Firstly, how's your hand, Sadé?' Mr Andrews asks.

'Much better. Thanks, sir,' I reply, but all I can focus on is our marks.

We crowd around Mr Andrews's desk and he tilts in his chair, smiling widely at us. He covers other people's grades up, so we don't see theirs.

But I see the one he's given us. It's an A-. We got an A for our presentation!

'Well done. You three had one of the highest marks in the class. Great content and experiment.'

'Yes!' Alfie pumps his fist.

Funmi grips on to my arm, while my stomach swoops around in circles like Nix when she gets excited.

'Here is your individual feedback – guard it with your hearts.'

Looking down at the slip of paper, I read words that no one but Mum has ever said to me.

Sadé, you're a natural storyteller! Your use of eye contact was effective throughout the presentation. You used a wide range of vocabulary related to the topic. You were clear and engaged well with your audience. Well done, Sadé!

Chapter Twenty-Four

Holding my journal, I draft lines for a new poem and doodle at the edges before closing my eyes.

* * *

I open them in my world, on the top of the cliff. Purple vines tangle through the ends of my hair.

'Today was the best, Nix.'

Nix circles me and makes a weird sneezing noise out of her nose, sending a spray of liquid at me.

'Yuck. Niiiiix,' I cringe, shaking the clear, gloopy gunk off my hands.

* * *

Someone falls on to the sofa beside me, I open my eyes.

Tolani punches my arm gently. 'Congrats on getting into the talent show. I knew you would.' She yawns. 'You're talented like Mum, you know.'

I play with the purple tassel of the journal as Tolani keeps talking.

'I used to be jealous of you and Mum because you both loved writing.'

Tolani was jealous of me?

I put my head on her shoulder. 'But you're so smart and good at everything.'

Tolani chuckles. 'Now, I didn't say anything about not being smart because we both know I am. It's just that you and Mum are . . . *were* so similar.'

Teni comes crashing down the stairs and plonks herself on Dad's reclining chair, still wearing her school uniform. 'Ashaunna said she spoke to you today. She said she's helping you with the talent show.'

'I've got my first practice with her tomorrow at lunch.'

'Can we see what you're performing?' Tolani asks.

My face warms from my sisters' eyes on me. I duck my head. 'It's not finished yet . . . I'm still changing parts of it. But I can read you another one?'

'Yes,' Tolani and Teni reply in unison.

Tolani continues, 'I mean. Only if you want to, I don't want you to feel forced into anything. My uni lecturer said that . . .'

Teni rolls her eyes at me, and I giggle, releasing some

of the nerves. Skimming through the filled pages of my journal, I choose my newest poem.

'I haven't finished it yet . . . but it's called *Memories*.

'Candy floss dreams lock
you to make believe,
Peppermint entwined,
Too permanent, too deep . . .'

The front door creaks open. I stop reading. Dad comes into the living room with a pinched expression. My sisters hold their breath.

'Finish the poem, Sadé,' he says softly. 'I want to hear the rest, please.'

Clearing my throat, I look at Teni for encouragement, before I look back down at my page, finding the line that I stopped at.

'Too permanent, too deep to leave,
Too sacred, too fixed to be set free,
Trapped smiles, caged breaths,
Stealing the air till there's nothing left,
But words, pictures and dusty clothes,
Trapped in a world where you never get old,
Only thing lasting is your colourful soul.'

Tolani throws her arm over my shoulder, sniffling softly. 'That was beautiful. Talented. Just like Mum,' she whispers, before pulling herself off the sofa.

Teni whispers, 'Shadz, I miss her too.'

Coughing, Dad quickly swipes the tears from his eyes. 'You remind me so much of your mum. My talented daughter.' He lets out a shaky breath, before leaving the living room.

* * *

I close my eyes again, entering my world. A weeping willow shields me as I work on my talent show poem, with Nix's head in my lap.

Chapter Twenty-Five

Wednesday

Sunny's body vibrates with laughter. 'Show me what Mr Sanders's face was like one more time.'

Concentrating, I squeeze my face together like Mr Sanders did when he saw I got the question right in lesson.

'Ah, man,' he says, grinning. 'If only I was there. Do you know how many times he's got me into trouble? Luckily my dad went to school with him, so he knows how miserable he can be.'

I can't imagine Mr Sanders young. I'm sure he was born in a sweater vest with a red pen in his hand and a disappointed look?

'What? Your dad went to school with Mr Sanders?'

'You should've seen his face at parents' evening when he realised who my dad was,' Sunny laughs. 'I didn't know he could get any redder. Apparently, my dad and Mr Sanders didn't get on at school. One time, my dad was put up against Mr Sanders in some kind of class debate and when my dad won, Mr Sanders lost it.' He laughs. 'He said the debate was rigged.'

Mr Sanders turning as red as a tomato materialises in my head and makes me laugh too.

Sliding over my latest homework, I ask Sunny, 'Can you check this for me, please? And also I can't stay for all of lunch today.'

Sunny clutches his chest and slumps on the table like he's dying. 'Traitor. You're ditching me after everything I've done for you. Like you don't care and you can go it alone. You're like Han Solo.'

'Who's Han Solo?'

Sunny groans. 'You're killing me, man. One of these days we're going to watch a Star Wars film. I can't have *my* mentee not knowing the greatest franchise to have ever existed and *no*, Marvel doesn't count.'

'Yeah, it does.'

Why does Sunny love Star Wars so much?

Holding his hand up, Sunny replies, 'I'm going to pretend that you didn't say that.' He flicks through my homework and swiftly marks the paper with his red pen. 'You're getting better. You remember the concepts, but it's the calculation part that throws you off.' Sunny chews his lip for a second, then stands. 'Wait here a second.'

My eyes follow Sunny across the room as he searches

through drawers until he pulls out some maths blocks, like the ones I used when I was younger.

Sunny comes back to the table, sits down and tears a piece of paper out of his book. He draws some lines and writes numbers alongside.

Sliding the paper over, Sunny says, 'I don't know why I didn't think of this before. There's something called dyscalculia. It's a condition, and people who have it can struggle with maths. These blocks and numbers lines will help you visualise things better. Show me how you would calculate this using the number line.'

I begin working out the maths problem Sunny suggested, and the number line *does* help me when I'm solving it. We try another and another, until I'm comfortable using it.

I notice the time and I'm already five minutes late to meet Ashaunna. As I'm shoving my book into my bag, I turn to Sunny.

'Sunny, you know what you said before about finding my thing. Poetry is *definitely* my thing.'

'The mentee has become the master!' Sunny bellows, drawing attention from the rest of the Learning Lab.

We high-five before I leave.

When I reach the library, Ashaunna is waiting for me by the entrance.

'Sorry I'm late,' I pant. 'I had Learning Lab.'

'With Sunny, right?'

I nod. 'You know Sunny?'

Ashaunna's white teeth glisten. 'Yeah, we're in the same classes. That guy is *so* funny, but he's obsessed with Star Wars.'

I giggle because she's right.

'Our study room is this way.'

I follow Ashaunna inside the library, passing the private spot where I sometimes sit for the support group, and we stop outside the Carver Room. The wooden door is shut, but we can see people sitting in the room through the small window.

'They're not supposed to be in there,' Ashaunna huffs. 'Let's go and check at the helpdesk. People like to steal other people's study rooms sometimes.'

We walk over to the main helpdesk.

'Excuse me, can I check my booking?' Ashaunna asks. 'We should be in the Carver Room, but there are people in there.'

The librarian closes his book. 'Can I have your name, please?' he asks.

'Ashaunna Michaels, that's Ash-a-u-n-n-a.'

He taps on his keyboard. 'Hmmm, you're right. I have you down here for the Carver Room so no one else should be inside.'

Coming out from his round book castle, the librarian

leads the way back to the study room, while pushing a trolley full of books ready to topple over.

He frowns. 'Wait. This isn't the Carver Room, it's the Seacole Room. What the . . .' The librarian pulls a sticky label off the bottom of his shoe. 'Hang on, I'll sort this.'

A single butterfly itches my neck. It feels like someone poured a cold can of Coke down my back. Fox's orange eyes glow in between the beige bookshelves. He doesn't come any closer.

'Thanks so much,' the librarian says, leading the other group out of our room. 'Sorry for the mix-up.'

Once the others have left, Ashaunna tucks her bag under her chair and sits down. 'The talent show is in two weeks, so we have time to go over the poem until it becomes natural. Can you read it out to me now?'

I nod, glad I stayed standing up.

Taking out my journal, I find the right page.

'Your stories are part of me, but I store more of you inside of me . . .'

Ashaunna stops me. 'You know the beginning without the journal, right?' she asks, and I nod. 'Let's start again, but without looking at the page. Relax, Sadé.'

I close my eyes and open them to my world.

* * *

My ears are flooded with familiar sounds of tweeting, chirping and squawking bursting from different directions. Tilting my head back, the warm wind rushes through my hair as I stare at the lilac candy floss sky. The clouds look fluffy today, like they could melt on my tongue.

'Your stories are part of me.' My voice echoes through my world, bending the willow trees before they bounce back.

'Your stories are part of me,
I store more of you inside of me,
See
your words photosynthesised –
breathed life.

My words don't make sense.
Should I deny you like Peter three times?
Deny, deny, deny
Give in to the lie.
Let the betrayal scar me
from the inside.'

Somewhere, someone clicks their fingers like they're at a real spoken-word night.

* * *

Ashaunna clicks her fingers together as if she's watching a poet perform, but it's only me standing here. I open my eyes.

'How did that feel?' she asks.

Like cold air rushing into my lungs. 'It felt good.'

'Let's try the rest. And, Sadé?'

I nod.

'Wherever you went just now? Go back there for your talent show performance – that's where your voice is.'

Chapter Twenty-Six

Friday

'I'll let you go early since you've all been great today,' Mr Sanders's replacement says, scratching his thinning grey hair. Mr Sanders didn't come in today and the rumours are flying.

'I heard Mr Sanders has chicken pox,' Alfie says, as we're packing up. 'All the times he makes those farty faces – I bet his bum was just itchy.'

'Ew,' Funmi replies, and Callum snickers.

Me and Funmi roll our eyes and hang back together as we walk out to the corridor. It's lunchtime. 'We added a new part to the dance,' she says. 'I can show you now if you want?'

Today is Friday so it's Ellie and *tell me how you're feeling* day. Lowering my voice so Callum can't hear me, I reply, 'Erm, I have that . . . thing today.'

Funmi squints for a second before realising what today is. 'That's cool. I can record the dance for you.' She looks down at her shoes. 'And . . . you can tell me about the *thing* after if you want.'

She meets my eyes and I smile at her. 'OK, yeah.'

I'm not looking where I'm going because I'm watching my friends walk down the corridor, and I crash into someone.

'Ouch!'

'Hi, Sadé,' Jas says, steadying me. 'Sorry for bumping into you. It's great you got into the talent show. Our group had to drop out because of my wrist.'

Ellie's session reminder flashes on my phone. 'Thanks, Jas. I hope your wrist feels better. I . . . I have to go now.'

'All right. Laters Sadé.'

Jas walks around me, but as she's leaving, I add, 'And I'm happy you're not friends with Trina any more.'

Jas turns back and grins widely at me. 'Me too.'

I reach Ellie's office. There's a ripped piece of paper stuck to the door:

Be back in five minutes ☺

After a few minutes, Ellie comes rushing round the corner with a tower of papers. 'Sorry, Sadé. Had to quickly pop somewhere. Go on in and tell me all about how your week's been.'

I hold the door open for her as she falls inside and dumps the papers on her desk.

'I got an A- in my science presentation *and* I got into the talent show.'

Ellie shrugs off her coat and hangs it on the pointy hook. 'That's amazing! Well done. What about the Learning Lab? How is that going?'

'Always remember, "your focus determines your reality", Sadé,' Sunny says. 'Qui-Gon Jinn was taken before his time. Can you believe they made him into a frigging voice in The Rise of Skywalker*? A voice!'*

'Sunny, what's this got to do with maths?'

'Everything!'

'Yeah, the Learning Lab is good too.'

'Well, I'm *extremely* happy to hear about all the amazing things happening on the outside, but I want to know what's happening in here.' She taps the side of her head. 'Let's talk about the support session for this week. Do you remember what it was about?'

'Yeah, it was about memories.'

'Bingo. I remember a few support sessions ago you'd mentioned the funeral not being a great way for you to say goodbye to your mum and I'd suggested that you think of something to do in memory of her. Any luck with that?'

'Yeah. I need my sisters to help me with it, but I think I've found a way that might work to remember Mum.'

'Great. You mentioned an older sister in the group. Can you tell me some more about your family?'

'Yeah, I was talking about my older sister Tolani, but I have another sister, Teni. Tolani is smart and Teni is cool and my dad . . . well, he's just my dad.' I shrug. 'And there's my grandma too, but she went back home to Nigeria like I said.'

'I know you mentioned your dad wasn't always great at listening. Has that improved at all?'

'Yeah. He said sorry and that he'll try harder.'

'I'm glad to hear that too. It seems like things are changing for the better.' Ellie smiles at me and then looks down at her notebook. 'And the second discussion question you chose was for you to finish a sentence off. *One of my biggest fears is . . .*'

'I – I just chose that one 'cos I ran out of time.'

'Do you want to finish it now?' Ellie asks. 'What would you say one of your biggest fears is?'

Just like that, I am back there again, listening on the stairs.

'Her grades are a cause for concern.'

'Please don't stress too much. You need to get some rest. Why don't you lie down, and I'll make you something to eat?'

Mum shook her head. 'I can't keep anything down – it'll just go to waste. We need to talk to Sadé. Why didn't she tell us she was struggling?'

Ellie tilts her head to one side. 'We can pass on this one for now, but I'll always be here when you are ready to talk about your fears.'

I have to face the beasts, there is no other way. But I don't know if I can.

Chapter Twenty-Seven

Sunday

It's Sunday morning and I can almost imagine Grandma's high-pitched singing outside my door, but she's not here. I'm trying not to think about what Ellie said about fears. I'm trying to forget all about mine.

Alfie and I are on a really hard level in *Deathless 2*. The zombies sink every time we throw a few quicksand paintballs at them, but then more appear.

Alfiedagreatest: nooo
more
OnceUponaTime: you still got the black hole paintball
Alfiedagreatest: yeah why?
OnceUponaTime: throw the ball in the middle
Alfiedagreatest: Yes! Next level
yes
nice one

no church today?

OnceUponaTime: I want to go but I don't wanna upset my dad

Alfiedagreatest: u can talk to him

you're the zombie queen

u can do anything

Sneaking downstairs so I don't wake up my sisters, I see Dad is already at the kitchen table with his newspaper and a fresh cup of coffee.

'Morning, Sadé,' Dad says, lowering his newspaper. 'Come and eat with me.'

'Thanks, Dad.' There's a plate of stacked akara and a steaming bowl of ogi opposite him just for me. Pulling out the chair, I sit down and stir the bowl of ogi, until Dad clears his throat, making me look up.

'What's wrong?' he asks, putting down his newspaper. 'Is your hand still hurting?'

'No, my hand's fine.' I nibble on a piece of akara. Then I take a deep breath. 'I know it's a bit late now, but can you drop us at church?'

Dad doesn't say anything for a while, so I think he's going to say no, but he nods instead.

'OK, but you need to wake up your sisters.'

As we get closer to the familiar stone church building, Dad's shoulders hunch over the steering wheel. I still can't believe Dad agreed to drop us. We thought he'd *never* want to come here ever again.

'Thanks for dropping us, Dad,' Tolani says from the passenger seat.

'I'm so tired, man.' Teni yawns beside me, half asleep.

Dad stops the car and turns around to talk to us. 'Have a nice time at church. I'll see you at home later.'

'Thanks, Dad,' we all say as we're leaving the car.

Looking back, I catch Dad staring after us, so I wave at him, and he waves back slowly, before starting the car.

As the heavy oak door squeaks open, everyone in the congregation turns to look at us at the entrance. I've missed the children's church because we're late.

Tolani cringes and pushes Teni forward. 'Teni, move in.'

In her rush, Tolani trips over someone's bag on the floor. She grabs on to Teni's leather jacket at the last minute and they both fall into empty chairs. I sit down next to them quietly.

Teni's top lip twitches and her shoulders tremble.

'Don't you dare laugh,' Tolani whispers harshly, not even a smile creeping on to her face.

Pastor Viv steps to the centre of the stage in a bold canary-yellow suit and clears her throat. 'Where was I?

As Christians, it's important to have faith and to believe that no matter what happens, God has your back. We already know that God will sort it out for us, but it's up to you to bridge the gap with faith. In those tough times, you have to have faith in God that he will help. With God, all things are possible . . .'

I wonder if my faith is large enough to fight off these beasts for good.

I wonder if it can also give me the confidence to perform my poem like I've been practising with Ashaunna.

'Let's pray. Thank you, Father, for all your children here today and those who couldn't make it here in person too. I pray that, in this coming week, they will exercise their faith in you and trust that with you . . . all things are possible. In Jesus's name we pray,' Pastor Viv calls.

'Amen!' the congregation calls back.

'Amen and amen. The service is now over.'

'I just need to talk to Auntie Grace about work and then we can go to Maccy D's,' Tolani says to me. 'You can get whatever you want.'

Yes!

Pastor Viv is sitting by herself at the front of the church.

My feet find their way over and I lower myself into the chair beside her.

'Hi, Pastor Viv.'

'How are you doing, Sadé?' she asks with a smile like a slice of soft, warm hard-dough bread comforting my insides.

If I could describe Pastor Viv as a colour, it would be a splash of yellow, orange, cyan and magenta all mixed together in a pot of brightness.

'I keep you and your family in my prayers. Sister Enitan is definitely missed around here. What's on your mind, Sadé?'

'My grandma says I should give all my worries to God and Ellie says that I need to work through my big feelings. What do you do when you're worried?'

She thinks for a moment. 'Well, your grandma is right and Ellie, whoever she is, knows what she's talking about too. Whenever I'm worried, I just remember that God will *never* give us more than we can handle. But he also doesn't leave us to face these big feelings alone. God knows what you can handle too, Sadé. We can then trust him to get us through the storm and into the sunshine.'

Pastor Viv's words settle in my mind like snow on a wintery night.

Someone waves to Pastor Viv from across the church. She signals to them to say she'll be right over, before turning back to me with her dough smile. 'Remember, my door and God's door are always open for a chat.'

'Thanks, Pastor Viv.'

* * *

Once we get home from church, I snuggle into the sofa with my steaming brown paper bag in one hand and my strawberry milkshake in the other. I swirl a handful of chips around in the milkshake before popping them in my mouth.

'That's *actually* disgusting,' Teni says.

Tolani winks, then does the exact same thing with her chocolate milkshake. 'Here.' She shoves the soggy chip in Teni's face, who pushes her hand away.

'Anyway, Shadz . . . How's that snitch group going?' Teni asks.

'It's *not* a snitch group,' I laugh. 'And it's good. Actually, there was something I wanted to ask you. Ellie said it would be good to find my own way to remember Mum. I think I've found one, but I'm gonna need your help.'

'Of course we'll help you,' Tolani says, and Teni nods in agreement.

'Can I have some of your milkshake?' Tolani asks, and drags a crooked chip through my strawberry cream and then her chocolate one before popping it in her mouth. 'Yum.'

I copy her.

'Yuck!' Teni yells. 'You're gonna make me sick.'

Me and Tolani crack up.

Tuesday

Grief Support Group Chat [5]

Ellie[moderator]: Welcome everyone! Anyone want to share how their week's been so far?

BendItLikeC: I went to tims exhibition

There was a picture of me in it

during a match

BendItLikeC shared a picture

BendItLikeC's face is covered, but it's a picture of them scoring a goal and the crowd cheering.

Anon05: sick

You'reDaObiWan4me: it's like when princess leia commanded the rebels

BendItLikeC: is that a good thing?

You'reDaObiWan4me: yeah

princess leia is the baddest

BendItLikeC: 🙂
Ellie[moderator]: Thanks for sharing with us @BendItLikeC! I'm glad you were able to go and remember Tim.

This is our penultimate session virtually. Next week will be our last session online.

Last week we looked at memories and today we're going to be discussing change and regrets. At the top of the screen, you should see a little basket. It's a Change Basket.

I want you to click on it and choose one or two items that you think symbolises something that has changed since the death of your loved one. Things like friendships, personality, family, responsibilities.

It will automatically pin to your name so everyone can see, so feel free to share. Any questions?
Anon05: do we have to do this
Ellie[moderator]: I'd like you to at least try. You have three minutes.

As I click on the basket, small pictures load up one by one, including a football, baseball cards, a teddy bear, a remote, a car, a hair clip, a book, a newspaper and a bracelet. What should I choose? Lots of things have changed.

In the end, I choose the newspaper, for New Dad, who is slowly becoming Old Dad again.

Ellie[moderator]: Time's up! Does anyone want to share what their item symbolises?
You'reDaObiWan4me: I don't need to talk about the slipper again
BendItLikeC: LOL
Anon05: im tired of hearing about dat slipper
Ellie[moderator]: and the temple?
You'reDaObiWan4me: mum is making us go temple more now
she thinks that our souls are damned because I joke about everything
Anon05: ur not even funny
Ellie[moderator]: Thanks for sharing @You'reDaObiWan4me. Anyone else?
BendItLikeC: I spend more time with my friends and fam now
tim thought life was too short
Ellie[moderator]: Thanks @BendItLikeC. I'm glad you're spending more time with friends

and family. Having a great support system around is so important. Who's next?

Anon05: ❤ for me

BendItLikeC: aww @Anon05 is in luv

Anon05: I gave up ciggies

promised my dad I'd give it up before he died

BendItLikeC: if I smoked I wouldn't be able to run half the field

good you gave it up

Ellie[moderator]: Thanks @Anon05. What about you @OnceUponaTime?

OnceUponaTime: 📰 for my dad

he was different after mum

BendItLikeC: what is he like now?

OnceUponaTime: more like Old Dad again 🙂

Ellie[moderator]: Thanks everyone. It's good to acknowledge that things have changed, and some things may never be the same, but it's also important to accept and figure out how to move forward with this new reality.

You're going to be creating your own change timelines today. You'll draw a line and mark the events of your life, from birth to now. You can draw or write any changes in – school, friends, family and homes.

It can be a curvy or straight line. I'll give you a few minutes for this one. You don't have to share it if you don't want to.

I select the paint tool and pick a wiggly line. I draw a baby face for my birth, a forest for when I first saw my world, the pointed tops of the school for when I moved to Hope Wood Secondary and then a sad face for when I started getting bad grades.

Ellie[moderator]: Two minutes left

I choose a cross for when Mum died and then a globe for when my world changed.

Ellie[moderator]: Time's up. I hope you managed to add in some important changes in your life. I won't ask you to share, but I wanted you to visually see that there is an element of loss connected to change. Many times, we think that it's only a death of someone that is linked with loss, but even losing a friend or moving house can affect a person. You may have been through many big changes in your life and it's perfectly fine to feel a sense of loss of those too – nothing is too minor.

Wherever you are. I want you to grab a piece of paper and write the word 'Regrets'.

Holding my journal down, I tear the paper as quietly as I can, but the sound rips through the library.

'Shuuush!'

Ellie[moderator]: I'm sure everyone has heard the word 'regret' before.

You'reDaObiWan4me: my dad regretted putting the expired mayo in his sandwich

the toilet also regretted it

BendItLikeC: LOOL

Ellie[moderator]: Thanks for that @You'reDaObiWan4me

You'reDaObiWan4me: any time

Ellie[moderator]: Regret. What does it mean to you? I recorded a little something for you all to listen to. Pop your headphones in . . .

Ellie's voice rushes through my headphones.

'Everyone has a regret or fifty, especially after a loved one has died. Did you get into a fight right before they passed? Did you promise

them something you couldn't fulfil? Do you feel like you let them down?

'The truth is, though, that nothing you did, said or thought caused the death of your loved one. So those regrets might not always be helpful to hang on to. Now, write your regrets down.'

Dad staggered into the living room, as if someone possessed his body.

'Dad, what's wrong?' Tolani asked. 'Did you miss visiting hours?'

'Your mum is gone,' he cried.

'Where did she go?' Tolani's voice wobbled. Then, 'She can't be gone. I'm seeing her tomorrow.'

Teni entered the room, as though sensing something wasn't right. 'Why does everyone look so sad?'

'Your mum is gone,' Dad repeated. 'Your mum . . . she . . . there were complications. She died.'

Ellie[moderator]: Now, I want you to draw or write your regrets down on that same piece of paper. I will give you a few minutes to do this.

As my pen hits the piece of paper, the blood rushes to my ears, but I don't stop. I keep on writing.

I wish I wasn't a cause for concern.

It was my fault Mum died.

I'm sorry that I didn't do better for her.

If I wasn't for me, my world wouldn't have changed.

Ellie[moderator]: It would be great if we could share one or more of our regrets, but you can pass as always.

BendItLikeC: I wish I had been there to save tim

Anon05: wish I didn't have a fight with my dad

Ellie[moderator]: Thank you so much for sharing and no worries if you didn't want to share on the chat. But all of you, if you are ready to let go of your regrets, I want you to tear up the paper and find a window. Throw the pieces of paper out of the window and let go. You're letting go of your regrets instead of keeping them trapped inside. After you let go of regret, you might want to explore gratitude and make a note of the things that you are thankful for about your loved ones.

I open the library window a crack. I tear and tear until my paper is in pieces. The tiny pieces fly, carried away on the sharp wind, joining other torn pieces of paper.

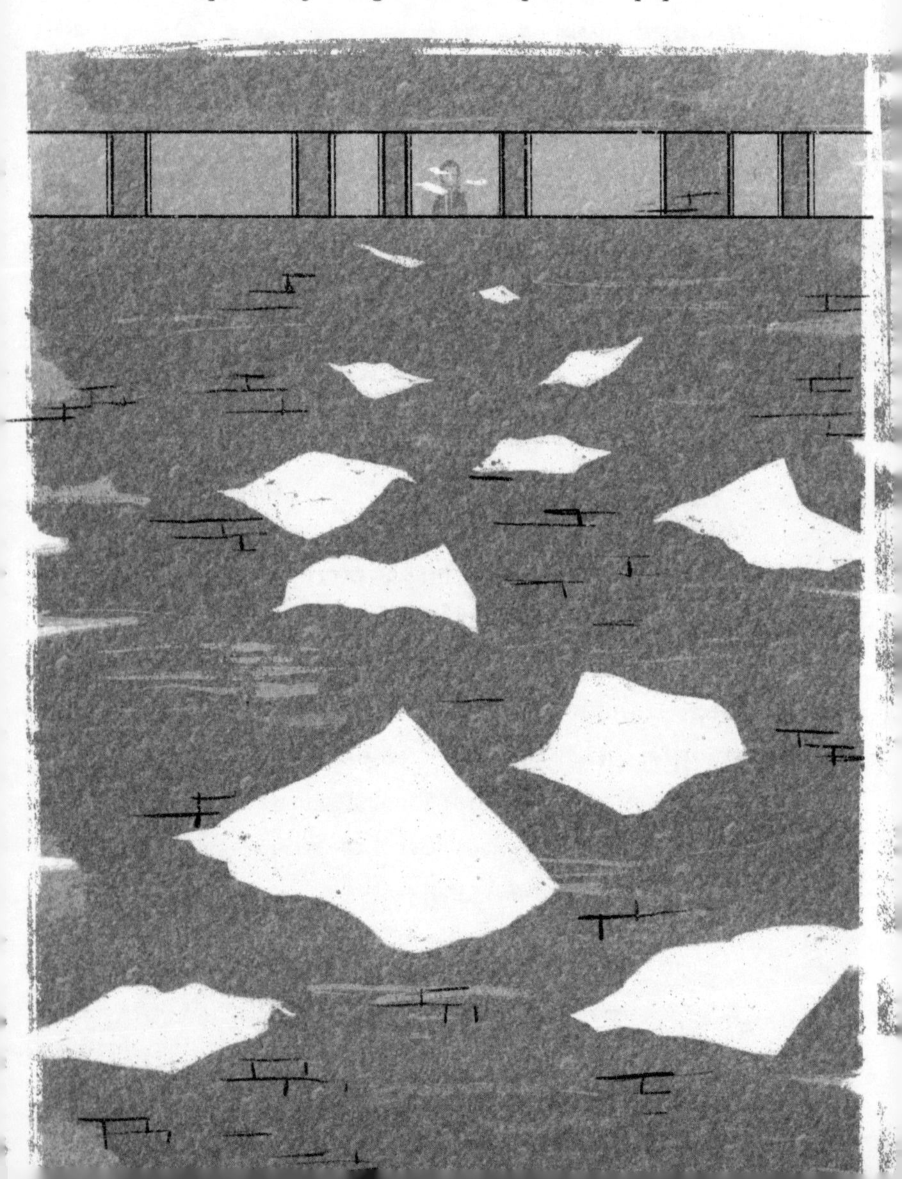

Then I find a fresh page and write:

Lurking like a nightmare –
ready to scare,
A dark cloud hanging over my
head,
You have no power here.

My words hold life,
Weakening your ties
the more I write,
Draining growls like a leak,
Clamping jaws, killing your fight.

Lurking like a nightmare
But you have no power – beware,
My words are beacons
guiding the good,
Destroying the dark, fighting the
fear
as they should.

Chapter Twenty-Eight

Wednesday

I keep on picturing my tiny pieces of paper blowing in wind. *You're letting go of your regrets instead of keeping them trapped inside.* Have I really let go of all my regrets?

'Newbie! Got the best seat in the Learning Lab reserved just for you. Prime seating.' Sunny fixes his glasses and kicks his feet up on the desk. 'You should be honoured. People pay to sit next to me.'

Sunny takes his feet off the desk and leans forward. 'Nothing? Not even a *little* smile. I'm giving you my best material here. Now, I've got a good one for you. "Impossible to see, the future is".'

'Ermm,' I reply, scratching my head.

Sunny groans at my confused look, running his hands down his face. 'Still? I drop these gems of genius *every* week and you still don't know. It's Yoda. I was saying, don't stress about the future.'

A pack of cards hit the table with a thud and Sunny starts sorting them. A pile for me and one for him.

'We can do maths another day. I'm not feeling it either.'

'But I need to—'

'. . . do it another day,' Sunny finishes my sentence.

'I wasn't gonna say that.'

'Yeah, I know, but let's think about it for a second. Maths.' He pretends to cry. 'Or cards. Whoo!'

'But . . . I don't know *how* to play.'

Sunny flips a card between his fingers. 'You're sitting across from a master. I'll be your sensei and teach you the art of poker.'

By the end of the Learning Lab, I've won. Sunny says it's beginner's luck, but I think he's just bad at poker.

Later, we're standing outside Mr Sander's class, when I see Jas struggling to lift her bandaged wrist to put her bag on.

'You need help with your bag?' I ask.

Jas stops struggling with her bag strap and turns around to look at me. 'Are we friends again?'

I shrug, holding Jas's bag strap so she can slot her arm through.

Gleaming gold charms dangle from Jas's bag; they reminds me of old times. 'I like your new charms. Do you remember when Natasha's brother used to sell jewellery from his car boot?'

Jas's eyes sparkle. 'He kept on saying it was top quality, but he got it from the pound shop.'

We giggle together.

Mr Sanders clears his throat and glares at us from the front of the line. 'We're almost at half-term so I don't expect to be kept waiting for silence. You should know how high my expectations are by now. Inside quickly and quietly.'

Funmi pulls on my arm and whispers. 'Sadé, have you seen the messages?'

'No talking!' Mr Sanders barks. 'That includes *you*, Funmi.'

'Someone shared one of your messages from your support group and some upper-schoolers were messaging about it.'

I rub at the growing pain my chest. 'What?'

'Isn't your username OnceUponaTime?' Funmi asks. 'Alfie told me that's the name you use when you guys play *Deathless 2*.'

'Funmi! *One* more word and I'll log you down for disruption of my lesson. You will have an hour's detention!'

What's going on?

I sit down, my stomach twisting like my cornrows. I feel like I'm on *The X Factor* and I've sung off-key.

'Check your phone,' Funmi mouths.

Bending down, my fingers shake and miss the zip a couple times. I grip the iPhone tight. Opening up WhatsApp, I see a screenshot. I recognise it right away. It's from the support group – when BendItLikeC was talking about going to Tim's exhibition.

OnceUponaTime: I went to see my mum to talk

sometimes I still imagine mum is speaking to me

BendItLikeC: what was that like

OnceUponaTime: sometimes

I see parts of her in other places

tim's thing could help you

a bit of him is there

BendItLikeC: maybe I will. I didn't think of that

Robbie: my mate said it's an anonymous grief support group at school

Lucy: who's your mate?

Jadyn: these kids are proper messed up man 😆

Lucy: who else is in the group? 🤔 I wonder what else they talk about

'Someone sent it to me,' Funmi murmurs.

Why would someone share this? Do people really think we're messed up? I hope they don't try to figure out who else is in the group.

I don't realise I'm crying until my lips taste like fish and chip Fridays. As my body curls deeper into the desk, I'm face to face with the dented table full of permanent scratches.

'Have you seen the screenshot?' Simone asks Trina. 'Do you think there are other secret groups in school?'

An arm falls over my shoulder and Alfie whispers in my ear. 'No one knows it's you in the message and I promise I won't tell anyone else. Zombie swear.'

Alfie holds out his pinkie finger and I wrap mine around his in a zombie swear. I instantly feel a bit better.

Mr Sanders morphs into the Kraken, terrorising the class. 'If I have to ask for silent working one more time, *all* of you will be in detention!'

The whispering stops. There's a knock at the door and a note is given to Mr Sanders by the same teaching assistant from weeks ago. I already know it's going to be for me.

'Sadé,' Mr Sanders calls. 'You're needed in Mrs Williams's office immediately.'

Part Four

The Battle

Chapter Twenty-Nine

After taking the longest way to Mrs Williams's office, I knock on the door, and I'm called in.

Ellie is here.

Tolani and Dad are here.

Mrs Williams gestures for me to come in and close the door. 'Thanks for coming, Sadé. Take a seat. Let's begin, shall we?' She sits and addresses the room. 'At approximately eight o'clock this morning, a screenshot from an anonymous school grief group was shared by one of its own members. The screenshot has since been circulated around the school. Ellie, would you like to . . .'

'Yes.' Ellie looks more frazzled than usual with her pink hair tied up. 'This was a very unfortunate occurrence, but it was not done with malicious intent. I have spoken to the student who shared the screenshot. They shared it to a friend to show how supportive and helpful the group has been. However, because they *did* break the rules, we've both agreed that they should leave the group for now and continue their counselling outside of the group.'

I look around. Tolani is looking anxiously at Dad, who looks bewildered. Leaning forward in his chair, Dad says, 'I'm sorry, I don't understand why we've been called in here. What has this all got to do with Sadé?'

'Mr Omotosho,' Ellie starts softly. 'It was messages between Sadé and the other student which were shared.'

With a rising voice and his bum half off his seat, Dad asks, 'What do you mean? My daughter isn't part of any grief group.'

'Dad. Let me explain—' Tolani starts.

Ellie pulls the elastic band out of her hair. 'Mr Omotosho, this is the grief support group Sadé joined at the start of term. You signed the consent form for her to be a part of it.'

'I did not sign anything,' Dad fumes. 'Can someone please tell me what's going on here?'

'Dad, don't be angry with me,' Tolani pleads, gripping the armrest. 'But I was the one who signed the permission slip for Sadé to be in the support group.'

He spins to face me, waiting for the truth, which he sees on my face. 'So you *have* been going to this support group?'

I hesitate for a second. 'Yes, Dad.'

Mrs Williams comes out from behind her throne with an apologetic look. 'I'm sorry, Mr Omotosho. I can assure you that the school knew nothing about this. We encouraged Sadé to join the group in good faith.'

Ignoring Mrs Williams's apology, Dad shifts in his seat and turns to Ellie. 'Can you tell me more about this group?'

'Of course,' she says. 'For the last five weeks, Sadé has been participating in a grief support chat and weekly one-on-one counselling sessions with me.'

Lifting himself off his chair, Dad shouts, 'Without my permission, Tolani! Why would you do this?'

Tolani shoots out of her seat, coming face to face with Dad. 'Sadé needed this—'

I close my eyes and I'm pulled into my world.

* * *

I am in the forest. Disorientated, I stumble deeper into the trees. The ground quivers at Lion's roar. Am I ready to face my beasts? I pick up my legs and sprint, jumping on the stepping stones, which raise me off the ground and light up a path to the Word Tunnel.

While Tiger sprints to the right of me, swiping her claws, Fox gallops to my left, taunting me.

'You can't run for ever.'

I know that Hen and Lion are behind me somewhere.

Vines grows through the ground and loop around my ankles. I tumble forward. Tiger springs in front of me, blocking my path, her sharp canines bared in a cruel snarl. Gripping on to a dangling vine, I swing over the beasts and drop down by the entrance of the Word Tunnel.

Diving into the tunnel, words bombard me from every angle as the beasts chase me.

Scared and forgotten like a rotten piece of gum glued under the desk.

My chest rises *1 . . . 2 . . . 3 . . . 4.*

It's me against grief, but it's not a fair match cos grief is a Casio calculator with all the answers. I'm failing.

I hold it in. *1 . . . 2 . . . 3 . . . 4.*

A poisonous
toad of a question. Feelings
cut me, the pain's deep, leaking memories
I can't keep.

And let it all go. *1 . . . 2 . . . 3 . . . 4.*

They don't know that you're reality and this world is the memory.

'Stop it!' I shout, bursting out of the tunnel straight into a swarm of bees.

They buzz all around me, blinding me so I can't see.

I trip and fall with a loud thump, which scares the birds from the trees. With my back against the ground, the beasts surround me, blocking out the soft lilac light.

'I didn't – I didn't do it,' I whisper.

My world groans and rumbles, the foundations shaking as if it's about to erupt.

'My grades *didn't* hurt my mum!' I shout. 'It's not my fault. It wasn't me!' My voice echoes across my world. The beasts are thrown back into the trees, and they hit the ground. The lilac sky illuminates, casting a bright glow over everything. It blinds me.

My breath comes out in puffs. I wipe the tears with my sleeve. I must've rubbed my eyes too hard because a weird wave of colour washes over my world, adding the last drop of colour my world needs.

The beasts have disappeared.

* * *

I feel someone hugging me and my eyes pop open. Tolani's arms are around me and her face is tucked into my neck. Over her head, Dad's eyes are intense puddles, full of more life than I've seen since Mum died. I drown out everything around me, but Ellie's voice seeps through.

'Mr Omotosho. With your permission, I would love to continue my counselling sessions with Sadé past the six-week period. I think she would benefit from it.'

Dad's eyes flicker to mine and I know the minute he has made up his mind. 'Yes, I think you're right.' He shifts in his chair to face Mrs Williams. 'I want to take my daughter out of school for the rest of the day if possible.'

'Oh, of course,' Mrs Williams rushes. 'I'll inform Sadé's teachers.'

Chapter Thirty

The crisp breeze from the open window of the bus bats against my face as Dad and me get off the bus. I still can't believe Mrs Williams let me go.

Dad keeps on checking his phone for directions. Turning right where the funny-shaped hedges live, we cross the road with the blinking lights. Once we get on to Manor Lane, I suddenly realise where we're going. I pat Oscar's furry Labrador head outside the newsagent's, and we wait for the green man.

Dad puts his hand on my shoulder as we get closer to the entrance of Hope Garden Centre. I thought I'd be sad coming here again, but instead I feel free.

The white stone steps have tall potted plants on either side, leading up to the welcome hut. It's as if I can hear Mum whispering in my ear.

'Are you ready to feed your imagination, Sadé?'

Yes, Mum. I am.

Dad looks down at me and takes my hand in his. 'I know your mum always brought you here. Can you show me around?'

A wide grin takes over my face. 'Thanks for bringing me back here, Dad. We can go to the tea house first. It has the best teas and cakes, *and* you can choose your own special tea.'

He makes a sound. 'Hmm, no coffee?'

Squeezing his hand back, I reply, 'They do very milky coffees too. You'll like it. And then after I can show you the greenhouse.'

Inside the entrance, a tall woman with skin the colour of peanut butter holds a large cactus in a pot. As she sees me, her eyes widen.

'Sadé, is that you?' she exclaims. She puts the cactus down and rushes over to give me a big hug, smothering me in her jasmine scent. 'I've missed you. How have you been?' She glances at Dad. 'Who's this?'

I squeeze Dad's hand. 'Hi, Cherry. I've missed you too. This is my dad.'

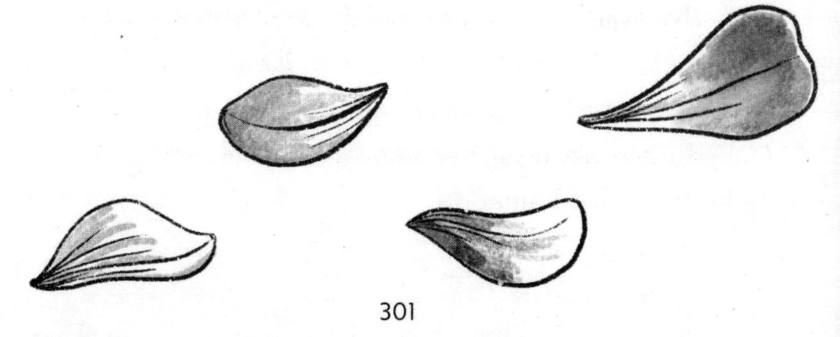

'Oh, it's lovely to meet you. I'm Cherry, the owner of Hope Garden Centre. I've missed my favourite customer!' She looks down at the cactus and then back at us. 'I need to give *this* to a customer.' She picks it up. 'I'll see you soon.'

The tea house is exactly how I remembered it, but instead of ordering peppermint tea for Mum and English breakfast for me, Dad and I choose one together. He doesn't want coffee after all.

We sip on spicy, rich, coppery cinnamon tea and chomp on warm buttery scones.

Afterwards, on our way to the greenhouse, we pass the bird shop, which is full of chirping in various pitches. There's a finch flying around with purple and orange colouring, just like Nix.

I tug Dad's hand towards the greenhouse, but he doesn't budge. His eyes remain fixed on the bird.

'I remember you telling me about a bird like that one. What was it called?'

Dad remembers Nix.

'Nix, Dad,' I say, my eyes wide. 'He's the bird from my world.'

Dad scratches the side of his head. 'Well, do you want the bird to take home?' he asks. 'You can only get it if you look after it, because—'

I don't let him finish before I'm hugging him. 'Yes, I promise I will, Dad. Thank you.'

Chapter Thirty-One

Thursday

My world is like it was before, including the Sanctuary, which is no longer ruined. Its extravagant stone structure stands strong in the centre of the forest.

I'm lying on my stomach in front of the rapping roses. 'I can't believe everything is back to normal.'

'Me too, Sadé,' Savannah replies gently.

Keith twists his stem around in excitement. 'We're back in the game.'

'And we've got something *new* for you.' Monica shakes and her strawberry petals flap up and down.

Savannah drops a beat and Keith smacks two leaves together, creating a clapping sound. I'm bounced in the air.

'We're sweeter than ever, stronger than ever,' he raps.

Monica's sleek voice comes in. *'We're spider's silk, yeah, you can't ever sever.'*

'You can't break us, we're germinating for ever,' Keith raps.

The beat and clapping stops.

'We've got your back, whatever the weather,' they all rap. *'Sadé, we've got your back, whatever the weather.'*

I laugh and dance in front of them. 'I've got your back, whatever the weather.'

* * *

'Why are you dancing?' Teni asks, and my eyes pop open. 'Get ready. You're coming to school with me today.'

'I think I'll stay here with Nix Junior,' I reply, thinking about everything that happened yesterday.

Teni pauses with a book in her hand. 'But Ashaunna was talking about practising with you today. Aren't you going?'

I forgot about our last practice. I can't miss it!

'OK, I'll go and get ready.' I jump out of my bed and whiz around the house like the Flash. I feel fine during the journey – but when I see the school building, my feet slow down.

Funmi is waiting for me outside. She takes one look at my face and gives a warm smile.

'Sadé, no one knows OnceUponaTime is you,' Funmi reassures me.

We walk down the corridor together. Stopping outside Mrs Karoma's room, Teni bends down, looking me straight in the eyes. 'Make sure you message if anything else happens, yeah?'

I nod, then go into the classroom.

'Last class we looked at some character diaries,' Mrs Karoma says. 'Today, we're going to explore characterisation in the play so far. You will each take one of the characters and write a short monologue from the point of view of that character. You'll then share your monologues within your groups as a conversation. Get into groups of four, please. I'll provide you with some character cards to help.'

'Can I join your group?' Jas asks, pulling up a chair.

I nod and smile at her. 'Yeah.'

Funmi nods in agreement. 'Sure. But I want to be Helena!'

She only wants to be Helena because everyone is in love with her in the play. I choose to be Hermia since Jas is Lysander and Alfie is Demetrius. Once our monologues are done, we stand in a circle to read them out.

'I love you, Lysander,' I say to Jas, before bursting into giggles. 'Why don't you love me any more?'

Jas takes a huge step away from me. 'Love!' She deepens her voice. 'The only woman I love is *her*.' She points at Funmi, who sways in her imaginary dress. 'Oh, beautiful Hermia. Marry me.'

Jas kneels down in front of Funmi and begs. It feels like my ears are going to burst from all the laughing.

'Get away, Lysander,' Funmi replies, stepping back. 'I love Demetrius.'

Alfie whips out an imaginary sword, jabbing it at Jas. 'Back off, Lysander. She's mine!'

Jas uses her good arm to block Alfie's sword and jabs her imaginary sword at him. 'Surrender, Demetrius, or face your death. Mwahaha . . .'

'Great group work, everyone! I hope you got to understand the main characters better.' Mrs Karoma grins. 'Pack away, please.'

Funmi nudges me and whispers. 'I like Jas again, now she's not under Trina's witchy spell.'

'Off you go!' Mrs Karoma calls.

As I'm on my way to meet Ashaunna inside the main hall, my phone vibrates in my pocket.

Grief Support Group Chat [6]

Ellie[moderator]: Hey everyone. I'm sure most of you have probably already seen or heard what has happened. A screenshot was taken from this group and it circulated around some of the students. I wanted to assure you that no other members' chat has been shared. I'm so sorry that this happened. I know one of our rules was confidentiality and your trust has been broken. One of our own members has been impacted by what happened and it's important to restore balance. I apologise again. We have decided together that it's best for @BendItLikeC to continue their counselling separate from the group. @BendItLikeC would like to say something.

BendItLikeC: I'm sorry @OnceUponaTime

I didn't know it would spread like that

I just wanted my friends to see how the group was helping me

@OnceUponaTime I'm really sorry

OnceUponaTime: that's OK

And I think it really might be.

Pushing open the main hall door slowly, I call. 'Hello? Ashaunna?'

Am I allowed in here?

'Sadé,' Ashaunna calls from the stage, and I jump. 'Come up here.'

I walk down the aisle of the empty hall. I've *never* seen it like this before! I can't believe that the next time I come here, it's going to be packed with people.

Joining Ashaunna on the wide stage, we look out at the empty auditorium.

As she swings to face me, the ends of her cornrows swing too so it's like the braids are flying. 'What do you see, Sadé?'

'What do I see?' I ask, confused. I squint at the empty hall. 'Er, nothing.'

Ashaunna laughs.

'It wasn't a trick question,' she says. 'There *isn't* anything to see, because no one's here. When I first started performing in front of bigger audiences, I would sometimes go to the venue when it was still empty. I want you to keep this exact image in your head for next week.'

'Is this like the thing where you imagine everyone in their pants? Because I don't really wanna imagine teachers in their pants.'

Ashaunna shivers. 'Yeah. No one wants to see that. Teni was telling me about everything that happened – with the screenshots, and your mum . . . Don't let any of that stuff get to you. How are you feeling about the show?'

A big smile comes on to my face. 'Good.'

'Remember that it's just you and your poetry – nothing else matters then. Now. Why don't you go from the beginning?'

Chapter Thirty-Two

Later on that day

As I'm feeding Nix Junior, Dad comes into the room and sits down at the edge of my bed.

'I heard you're doing a talent show next week,' he says.

My eyes go as round as a pound coin. 'Who told you?'

'Tolani,' we say at the same time, and laugh.

Dad clears his throat and fixes the collar of his burgundy dressing gown. 'Your mum would be so proud of you if she was here.'

I'm doing something like Mum would.

Flying like Mum would, a gliding kite of words spiralling across the page, leaving nothing locked up. Speaking free of the cage.

Dad's large hands grasp on to my ankle and shake it. I giggle. Once Dad stops, I ask him the question that's been stuck in my head. 'And you're sure about me going to the last support group session? And seeing Ellie on my own afterwards?'

Dad sighs deeply. 'Hmmm, I'm still not convinced. You know how I feel about therapists. They're always in your business and want to know all your secrets – but it seems to be helping you.'

Flying across the bed, I hug my dad and he pats my back. Once he leaves the room, I take out my journal and read over my talent show poem. I can't believe it's finally happening next week. If Mum were here now, I know we would be practising together.

I enter her peppermint-filled study, picturing what it would be like. Tracing Mum's special box with my fingertips, I pull out a piece of paper with her scribblings all over it. Mum thought stories should be told, but she started writing them down just for me. She never got to finish it. I was scared to look before because it would mean Mum was really gone but now I want to.

In the great kingdom of Lekki, Tiger's family were known for their prowess and strength. Her parents were champions and named 'strongest in the land'. Tiger was known for her smarts, but she wanted to be known as 'strongest in the land' too. She enlisted the help of people from her town.

First, she went to Maxim, a well-known farmer, for help.

'Maxim,' Tiger said. 'Put your largest yams into a wide bucket. I bet I can lift it twenty times.'

Maxim was fond of Tiger and didn't want to discourage her, so he agreed. While she warmed up, Maxim cut out the middle of all the yams and glued them back together. You see, the inside was what made the yams heavy.

'Here you are,' Maxim said. 'A wide bucket and my largest yams, as strong as you are.'

Tiger lifted the bucket easily twenty times over her head and she thought that soon she'd be known as strongest in the land too.

Next, Tiger went to Brianne, the finest craftswoman in all the land, and asked if she could weave a strong rope for her. Once she was done, Tiger asked Brianne to gather three others for a game of tug-of-war.

Brianne was fond of Tiger too and didn't want to discourage her, so she agreed. While Tiger warmed up, Brianne gathered three people and greased their hands. Tiger faced up against the four in a game of tug-of-war. They pulled and the rope slid through their hands. Tiger thought that soon she'd be known as strongest in the land.

She tested her strength, and all helped her because they were fond of her. But her friend, Lion, knew what the people were doing wasn't right because they weren't telling Tiger the truth.

'Tiger,' he said. 'These people are being kind to you. But you are not the strongest in the land – you have the strongest mind in the land, instead.'

Tiger couldn't see sense and she didn't believe him. Tiger didn't want to be known as the 'strongest mind in the land', but 'strongest in the land'.

She went back to Maxim to prove Lion wrong. As she arrived, Maxim was frying some yams. The pan caught on fire. He became trapped behind a heavy beam and couldn't escape. Tiger, who thought she was the strongest in the land, lifted, pushed and pulled, but she couldn't get Maxim free.

Then she remembered something she'd read.

'Maxim,' she said. 'Grab a towel and wet it and throw it over the fire.'

Maxim was fond of Tiger and so he did what she said. After a few tries, indeed the fire was dead.

Tiger accepted the truth, for it was right. She may not have been the strongest in the land, but she knew her brain would win in a fight.

I miss all her stories. Digging through the box, I search for more, but I find an envelope with my name on it instead.

To Sadé, my darling daughter,

I know you'll find this letter because these stories are as much a part of you as I am. The stories belong to you, but the words that matter most are your own. How is that world of yours? One thing I'll miss the most is you telling me about Nix, your rapping roses and the candy floss clouds. If only I could taste some of that sweetness. Your dad said he wanted to bring me his 'one in town' fried rice, but I only want to taste it when I'm back home with you all.

Don't ever let go of that amazing imagination, Sadé, and that God-given gift you have. Your words are powerful. Don't let anyone silence you or tell you that your words aren't enough, because they are. I'll always be where you are. I can't tell you how much your words and your world have made me feel better.

Wherever you need me, that's where I'll be.

Mum x

Chapter Thirty-Three

Monday

Stomping feet and clapping hands rattle the hall and shake my brain as we watch from behind the curtains. I spot Ashaunna in the audience and my stomach dips like when Nix is flying near the bubble sea.

'Let's give them a round of applause!' Mr Lawrence yells, jogging up and down the stage after the first performance is over.

Funmi dances around on the spot. 'I'm too excited.'

Closing my eyes and shutting out the world and Funmi, I mumble the lines of my poem to myself over and over.

God, please let me get this right. Please don't make me a meme.

'Before we have our second dance act of the night, we have a poet called Sadé and let me tell you she's ah-mazing. Let's have a round of applause for Sadé as she comes to the stage.'

Funmi squeezes my arm in encouragement. I step on

to the stage. My eyes scan the large audience, as I try to stop shaking. The mic feels heavy in my hand.

A single butterfly flutters through the crowd and lands right at the foot of the stage. I can't hear the audience any more. The familiar cold chill trickles down my spine, until all my hairs are sticking up. I can only hear the pounding of my heart because I know what comes next.

The beasts. I thought they were gone for good!

The beasts burst in from the high windows of the hall. They're five or six feet tall, looming over me.

In.

1 . . . 2 . . . 3 . . . 4

Exactly how I've been taught. I squeeze my eyes together.

Death and life are in the power of the tongue. Mum's voice soothes me like mint.

'You're *not* in control,' I mutter.

Lion roars.

'We'll see about that,' Fox smirks.

Instead of going into my world, I bring the vibrancy of my world into the ordinary school hall. The candy floss smell fills the hall, wrapping me up in a warm hug. There's a loud squawk and Nix rockets over the audience with her wings spread as wide as a plane.

I open my eyes.

'My poem is called "The Beasts Inside" and it's about my mum.'

'Your stories are part of me,
I store more of you inside of me,
See
your words photosynthesised –
breathed life.'

My voice echoes across the hall through the mic and the beasts are pushed back by a strong wind. Tiger fights against it with a growl, snarling in my face. Vines grow out from the walls and trap her arms behind her back.

'My words don't make sense.
Should I deny you like Peter three times?
Deny, deny, deny
give in to the lie;
let the betrayal scar me
from the inside.

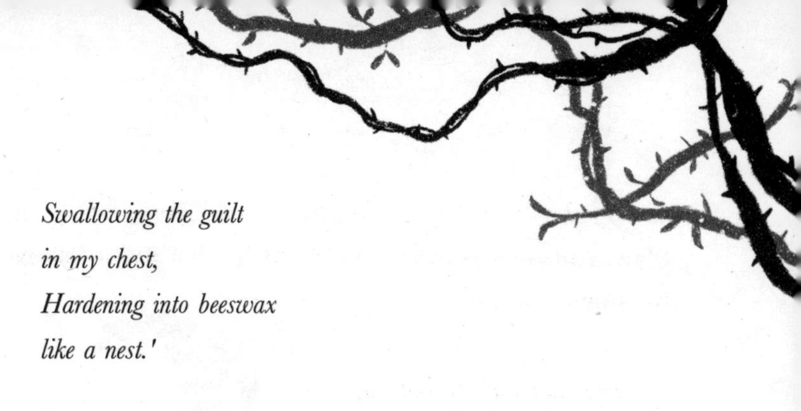

Swallowing the guilt
in my chest,
Hardening into beeswax
like a nest.'

My crowd-surfing grass springs up. Hen clucks and hops towards me, dodging the grass, but the thorns grow, tangling around her claws and bring her down.

'They say I have to let go
like a kite, let go,
Like a flight, let go,
Spirit fly, let go.

Are my words powerful enough to keep
buried deep
and
wake you from your sleep?
This isn't a fairy tale,
There's no prince.
Ever since that day,
I've wanted this nightmare to end.
We can pretend and start again.'

My muttering moths swarm around Fox's head. He snaps at them with his needle-like teeth, but they continue swarming Fox until he can't see.

'Anger eats me like a
hungry caterpillar,
Cocooned words
unsaid,
Wings trapped,
The words expired
past the date.
I could have
rehearsed;
practised being sad,
Sadness is all I have.'

Lion's jaws open so wide that I think he might devour me whole, but I keep going.

'This nightmare must end,
We can pretend and start again.
Mum.
Let's start again.'

The beasts are blasted back again as my words wash over them. Gone are the scary red eyes of Tiger; instead they are back to warm yellow. Hen's silky feathers are back, and Fox is on all fours. Lion's deep grooves have smoothed out.

'Thank you so much, Sadé,' Mr Lawrence says.

Running off the stage with the energy still pumping through my veins, I don't know what my friends are saying, but I do see grins and hear cheers.

'Last up we have a dance group called the Elite Dancers.'

I stumble back to my seat at the front of the hall with a smile as large as Canada on my face. Funmi and the twins jump on to the stage, the beat pulsating throughout the hall. As their arms pump and their legs kick, people shout, and the moment clicks. The last beat drops. Standing up, I clap along cheering them on.

'Woooo!' Mr Lawrence cheers. 'What an ah-mazing show. One more round of applause for everyone who participated today.' He waits for the crowd to settle down before speaking again. 'We have some truly talented students at Hope Wood Secondary! Please take your seats and get out your phones. It's time to cast your votes! As usual, please vote for your first, second and third choice. And don't forget, we have an extra category this year for a "crowd favourite". For those who don't have access to a device, please ask the ushers at the sides.' He points at the upper-schoolers on either side. 'You will be able to vote on one of the iPads.'

My fingers fumble as I take out my phone. I still can't believe I did it. Scrolling down to the bottom, I choose Elite Dancers from the list. I hope my friends win.

Mr Lawrence snaps his fingers together quickly. Two lower-schoolers stumble on to the stage carrying a small white table. They scurry off, coming back two seconds later with their arms full of trophies, envelopes and a big basket.

Could one of those be for me?

'I wonder who's gonna win,' Funmi whispers beside me. 'I want us to win something. Did you see everyone clapping for us?'

'I can't believe we did it,' I whisper back.

Mr Lawrence taps on the mic and the noise dies down. 'And the votes are in!'

He taps on his iPad repeatedly before sighing and gazing up at the ceiling. A few people laugh because Mr Lawrence is always so dramatic. One of the lower-schoolers trips on to the stage with a new iPad which Mr Lawrence snatches out of his hand.

'Sorry about that! We're going to start off with third place. Can I get a "whoa"?'

'Whoaaaaaaaaaa!' the crowd roars.

'And third place goes to . . . Elite Dancers. Come on up!'

My friends' screams almost pop my ears. They run up the side steps. Funmi obviously pushes to be first on stage. As Mr Lawrence hands them their trophies, his assistant passes them a white envelope each and Funmi tears hers open.

'They each get . . . lunchtime tokenssss! Well done, ladies.'

'And second place goes to . . . Can I get a woah?'

'Whoaaaaaaaaaa!'

'Michael with his amazing keyboard and drums performance!'

Michael rushes up, beating the stairs with his drumsticks.

'And he gets a free meal at Nando's! Great stuff, Michael! And the winner is . . .'

'WHOAAA!'

'Red Rosesssss! Get up here, ladies!'

'Your a cappella was perfection! You each get a thirty-pound Westfield voucher.'

The girls jump up and down. My stomach dips a little, but I'm still happy I did it.

'Thank you to all our winners! Now, we have one final vote to announce. It's new and sparkling. It's the crowd favourite vote. Can I get a "woop-woop"?'

'Woop-woop!'

'And the crowd favourite vote goes to . . . Sadé, for her ah-mazing poem!'

Is he saying *my* name?

'Yes, Sadé!' Teni screams.

The purple butterflies trapped in my stomach flutter around. Funmi is signalling for me to come up.

I float up the stairs and Mr Lawrence hands me my trophy. Turning it over in my hand, it doesn't feel real. None of this does.

'Here is your gift basket filled with goodies. Your poem was per-fection!'

We get one more cheer and then head back to our seats. I'm carrying the hefty basket filled with sweets, chocolates and a pair of headphones.

'And that is the end of our show for tonight. I hope you've enjoyed it because I certainly have!' Mr Lawrence hollers into the mic. 'Good night.'

We file out of the hall and we're standing outside. There's a strange buzz in the air and my skin feels like it's sparking. My phone vibrates in my pocket. Taking it out, I see Grandma is video-calling me.

'Hi, Grandma!'

Grandma's forehead covers the camera. 'Omo mi. How are you?'

I laugh. 'I'm fine, Grandma, but I can't see your face.'

There's some rustling before Grandma's golden-brown skin, now the colour of toffee from the Nigerian heat, appears on the screen.

'I can see you now.'

'Good. Teniola sent me the recording of your talent show just now. My talented girl.'

I didn't even know that Teni was recording me. 'Thank you, Grandma.'

'Aro re n so mi pupo. Mo fẹ pe mo le wa nibẹ pelu e.'

I miss you so much. I wish I could be there with you.

'Me too,' I reply, touching the golden locket around my neck. 'I need to go now, we're all going to celebrate. Bye, Grandma.'

Someone clears their throat behind me. 'Sadé.'

Mr Sanders is standing there. I hope he's not going to talk to me about my maths grade. Not even my grades can ruin this day.

'Yes, sir.'

Mr Sanders straightens his blue sweater vest. 'Your poem was . . . good. It was *very* good,' he says, with an unreadable expression on his face.

'Thanks, sir. Poetry is kinda my thing.'

Tuesday

Grief Support Group Chat [7]

Ellie[moderator]: Welcome everyone! This will be our last chat online. I wanted to check in and share the details for our in-person session at the end of the week. As always, if you're not comfortable with meeting, please let me know.

I can't believe I'm going to meet all of them. I wonder if they'll be the same in person.

Anon05: I have to hear dead jokes in person @You'reDaObiWan4me
You'reDaObiWan4me: LOL you love my jokes just admit it
Ellie[moderator]: It will be great to see all of you. Our session will be in Hope Wood's sensory garden.
OnceUponaTime: we have a sensory garden?
Ellie[moderator]: Yes! Mrs Williams allowed me

to turn the extra piece of land into a garden just behind the sports hall. It's like the Hope Garden Centre you spoke about.

Anon05: the ice queen agreed

u give her your kidney

Ellie[moderator]: I can confirm that I still have both of my kidneys. Mrs Williams saw the benefits of a sensory garden for those in counselling.

You'reDaObiWan4me: sensory gardens are good for stress release and cognition

Anon05: cheers google

Ellie[moderator]: **@You'reDaObiWan4me** you are very right. Does anyone have anything else to add?

OnceUponaTime: I have something to say

I think BendItLikeC should come back

Ellie[moderator]: **@OnceUponaTime** that is very mature of you! What do the rest of you think?

Anon05: yh bring them back

You'reDaObiWan4me: I concur

Ellie[moderator]: Thanks everyone. Then it is settled, BendItLikeC will rejoin the group. If no one has any questions, I will see you at the end of the week.

Chapter Thirty-Four

Friday

I push through the thick, prickly bushes and come out into the sensory garden. The strong fruity smell of honeysuckle mixed with lavender hits my nose. Water trickles down the mini waterfall in the corner, creating a plop sound every few seconds. Brightly coloured flowers fill the garden. Ellie is in the centre by the rows of empty flower beds, while the others sit on wooden benches.

'Sunny?'

Sunny lifts his head, grinning widely at me. 'Newbie! Or should I say, *OnceUponaTime*. I should've guessed it. The clues were right there!'

'Hi, Sadé, good to see you,' Ellie says. 'You can grab the seat by Dylan or Sunny.'

Dylan turns around and I can't believe it! Dylan is my upper-schooler secret-spot stealer. With his hands stuffed into his pockets and a grin, he asks, 'Found any more good spots?'

With a matching grin on my face, I shake my head. 'Not yet.'

'We're just waiting for one more person,' Ellie says. 'Oh, here she comes.'

Charlie emerges from the bushes with her blonde hair scraped back into a tight ponytail.

'Perfect, everyone is here,' Ellie says. 'Let's go around the table and you can introduce yourselves officially.'

Sunny taps an imaginary mic like he's at a comedy show. 'Welcome to the stage, You'reDaObiWan4me – or, Sunny.'

'Booo,' Dylan interrupts.

Sunny chucks his empty cup at Dylan, who ducks just in time with a chuckle. 'Obi-Wan Kenobi was a master! "Anon05" isn't any better.'

Ellie quirks her eyebrow at Sunny and Dylan. 'The rules we had online still apply now.'

Charlie lifts her chin in greeting. 'I'm BendItLikeC. The "c" is for "Charlotte", but no one calls me that. It's just Charlie.'

Once Dylan introduces himself, it's my turn.

'My name is Sadé and I'm OnceUponaTime because I love to write.'

'Congrats again for the talent show, Sadé,' Ellie beams, and the others congratulate me too.

Charlie says, 'I know I've said it already, but I'm really sorry for the whole screenshotting thing, Sadé.'

By the end of the week, everyone had forgotten about the screenshots and all they could talk about was the talent show.

'It doesn't matter,' I reply, and I mean it.

'Great,' Ellie says. 'Now we've all been introduced. I hope everyone is ready to do some gardening and we'll have some time to chat too.'

We're all handed a pair of too-big gardening gloves like the ones Cherry wears as we gather by the raised garden beds.

A bee smelling the lavender buzzes around Charlie's ear. She runs away from it, which makes it chase her.

'You have to stay still, or you'll scare it,' I tell her. 'Pretend you're a statue.'

Charlie stands still for a few seconds and the bee takes off to sit on a flower.

'Nice one, newbie.' Sunny shoots me with fake lasers. 'Did you know that a queen bee can produce two thousand eggs a day?'

Dylan pokes at his piece of land with a stick. 'Gross,' he mumbles.

Ellie kneels to tend to her soil, and we do the same. 'We're going to talk about our help circle and what helps us with grief. Having a support system is very important. Families can help you a lot, but there are other people who are not as close – teachers or friends, for example – who can help too.'

Using her finger, Ellie draws a large round circle in the soil and smaller rings inside. 'Imagine this is your help circle. While you prepare your soil, think about who would be in your help circle.'

As I drag the small rake across the wet soil, I think about my help circle and touch the locket around my neck. My family: Grandma, dad, Teni, Tolly. My friends: Alfie, Funmi, Callum . . . and Jas. This group: Ellie, Charlie, Sunny and Dylan. And my church, especially Pastor Viv, and God. And Cherry at Hope Garden Centre, and my nice teachers, and Nix Junior.

Ellie points at my soil. 'Looking good, Sadé.'

'Why does yours look better than mine?' Charlie asks Sunny.

Sunny laughs. 'Because your raking technique is all wrong.' He shows her how it's done.

Ellie rubs her gloves together to shake off the soil. 'Let's talk. Who's been helpful to you during this time?'

'Dan from the batting cages. He doesn't talk much, but he lets me bat for free,' Dylan replies, stabbing at his soil.

'That's like my coach,' Charlie adds. 'He lets me stay on the field after games sometimes.'

'Thanks, Charlie and Dylan. What about the rest of you? Do you have someone who's helped you?'

'My friends, God, family and fighting all those zombies,' I answer, thinking about the last game Alfie and I played.

'Are you talking about *Deathless 2*?' Dylan asks. 'I'm stuck on Level Fifty.'

'"Night of the Fallen"!' I exclaim. 'You need to hide behind the barrels. When all the zombies come, hold down the master key and it squashes them with the barrels. Takes them all out. That's why the level is called—'

'"Night of the Fallen",' Dylan finishes with a chuckle.

He reaches for his phone, but Ellie coughs and gives him a look. 'You can fight all the zombies you want *after* this session. So, Sunny, who has helped you?'

'You guys helped.' Sunny clicks and points at us. 'We're like the Rebel Alliance from *Star Wars*. I guess it's a bit different because their goal is to fix the Republic.'

'Why are you always talking about *Star Wars*?' Dylan's face probably matches mine. 'It's boring.'

Sunny chucks his rake down. 'You think *Star Wars* is

boring? It's rumoured that C-3PO can speak over *six million* languages and there are creatures that can live for thousands of years. How can you get any better than that?'

Ellie shakes her head, a small smile on her face. 'Thanks for enlightening us on the greatness of *Star Wars*, Sunny. In one of our sessions, we spoke about things we can do to help us when we're upset, such as playing football, as Charlie said. We're not going to be meeting in a group like this any more, so just think about things that can help you cope moving forward.'

Ellie shows us how to dig and plant our seeds. I dig a narrow ditch in the soil and shake the bag of sunflower seeds into it, using the tip of my finger to make sure they're spread apart. I pile the soil back over and water it.

'I see most of you have planted your seeds.' Ellie inspects our work. 'I can't wait to see them grow. It's really something to see a plant flourish. I want you all to think about how *you've* grown over these last six weeks. Sadé, you're more confident; Sunny, your support system has grown; Charlie, you're learning to let go; and, Dylan, you're more open.'

'Arh-wooooooooo!' Sunny howls.

Dylan bursts out laughing.

Ellie leaves us for a few minutes to wander around the

sensory garden and reflect on our own. I find a comfortable bench hidden in the corner. Sitting down, I close my eyes and enter my world.

* * *

When I open my eyes, Mum is waiting for me on the cliff. I think about what she said in her letter. *Wherever you need me, that's where I'll be.*

'My darling daughter. Come and sit with me.'

The huge botanical fist cradles Mum and me as we look out over my world. My colourful world.

'Just look at the world you created, Sadé.' She spreads her arms wide.

'Where did you go?' I ask. 'I couldn't find you for ages.'

She squeezes my shoulders. 'Go? I've always been here, but you stopped seeing me because of what you believed.' Mum takes my face in her hands, squeezing my cheeks together. I always hated it when she did that, but I don't mind much now. 'You know it wasn't your fault what happened to me.'

I nod and she lets go of my cheeks.

'And I know I'm not in your normal world any more, but you have your sisters and your dad. I know they'll take good care of you. Can you do something for me?' Mum asks.

'Anything,' I reply, clinging on to Mum's peppermint smell.

'I've started a new story and I want you to finish it for me.'

Mum wraps her arm around my shoulders and my head drops to her chest. 'Once upon a time . . .'

Epilogue

Mum's study door is slightly open. Pushing it open, I find Dad sitting at Mum's desk, looking out of the window.

'Dad, are you coming with us?' I ask.

He smiles. 'I wouldn't miss it – but I'll meet you there.'

I turn back before closing the door softly behind me. 'Ellie said it's important for me to find my own way to say goodbye to Mum. You can find your own way to remember Mum too.'

I go downstairs. A small stack of Dad's letters is piled on the table beside the door. One of the letters is from school. It's probably my report card – Mr Andrews said it would be going out this week. It doesn't matter anyway, not like it did before because I tried and did my best.

'Sadé, are you ready for this?' Tolani asks, putting on her coat.

I put the envelope back down. 'Yeah, I'm ready.'

We walk past the bus stop, turning right where the funny-shaped hedges live and cross the road with the blinking lights. After we turn left on Manor Lane, I pat Oscar's furry head outside the newsagent's, and we wait for the green man.

Funmi, Alfie and Jas wave from across the road and shout my name for us to join them. As I reach the other side, Pan barks and pounds across the pavement with his pink tongue flopping about. Dropping to the ground, I hug his shiny black fur coat and his wet tongue tickles my hand.

Teni wrinkles her nose. 'Make sure you wash that hand, yeah.'

I take Pan's lead and walk him over to Alfie, Funmi and Jas wait for me, before smothering me in a four-way hug.

Alfie holds up the chewed dog leash. 'Paaaan – not again. Mum's gonna kill me. This was his third leash this month.'

Pan's tail flops around as he leaps to catch a flying moth. Alfie is wearing his new red Hope Garden Centre T-shirt.

After his sweets business failed, Alfie was serious about not getting into trouble any more. I noticed that Hope Garden Centre were looking to pay young helpers in the stock room, so now he can get Hailey her present without worrying about getting his fiftieth detention with Mrs Williams.

Charlie appears out of nowhere, dribbling a ball. Forgetting about me, Alfie darts towards her, attempting and failing to steal the ball from her.

'Come on, Alfie!' she laughs, and he chases her inside.

Pan yaps excitedly and we follow them through the Hope Garden Centre entrance all the way to the reading area at the back with the bean bags and funky chairs.

There's a small crowd already seated, and my friends join them on the remaining mats. My palms sweat. *I didn't know so many people would come!*

Moving through the crowd, I say hello to people I haven't seen in months. Regulars at Hope Garden Centre who my mum read to and wowed with her stories. Pastor Viv is here! And she's wearing one of her bright-green suits.

'Newbie!' Sunny shouts from the middle row.

I wave, motioning with an invisible lightsabre. Dylan shoves Sunny with his shoulder and they slap-fight. Charlie sits in between them to stop them fighting.

I walk up to the front and Cherry pulls me into a tight jasmine-filled hug. 'You're here,' she whispers. 'Are you good to go?'

'Yeah,' I reply.

Shifting in the huge, white teardrop chair facing the audience, I clasp my purple journal with both of my hands and nod, looking down at the page to remind me of the story.

When I look up, I see a bright-pink fringe approaching as Ellie sits next to the rest of the support group. Ashaunna runs in after her, out of breath, and hugs Teni, before squeezing on the mat next to her.

Cherry sits at the front with her legs crossed. 'Great, let's get started.' She settles the crowd. 'Thanks, everyone, for coming to support Sadé.'

Everyone gives a gentle round of applause.

I take a deep breath. *1 . . . 2 . . . 3 . . . 4.*

'I'm going to be reading my mum's stories. The stories she never got to finish writing, but I did – just for her.'

Teni and Tolani are smiling proudly at me, and whenever someone starts talking, they both give them looks. Teni turns the phone towards me, and I see Grandma waving back all the way from Nigeria. I touch my locket.

This is my way to remember.

Clearing my throat, I look out into the crowd one more time. I still can't believe they all came for me.

I look back down, and my finger skims the first sentence. 'Once upon a time—'

Out of the corner of my eye, I see Dad coming in at the back. He is holding three bunches of yellow sunflowers in his hands.

I guess he found his own way to remember Mum too.

THE END

Mum's Stories

Lion's Story

'Once upon a time, there were two market sellers who could not have been more different. You had the scheming Fox and the generous Tiger, who always did what was right. The cunning Fox would charge high for a coconut but scoop out the insides and his customers had to pay twice. Tiger would give her sweet fruit to those in need.

'One day, Lion sent his men to buy fruit for him, and Fox's fake fruit filled the bags to the brim. Lion roared when he broke open his empty treats because he was hungry, and he had nothing to eat.

'Lion had heard about the generous Tiger and her amazing stall; Tiger made the prince a feast as wide as a wall. Lion ordered Fox to repay the whole village and awarded Tiger with a Chief Seller plaque.'

'Ooh, I know what this story means!' Tolani shouts out like Alfie in class. 'During one of my uni lectures—'

Teni kisses her teeth. 'Just say what it means.'

I hide my smile. 'What do you think it means, Tolly?'

'That it's not good to be deceitful, and things that you do in secret will eventually come to light.'

Hen's Story

'Once upon a time, on the first day of the wet season, the rich village of Ado nominated a town crier. Hen was widely known for her loud "cock-a-doodle-doo". She crowed early in the morning, at the market and at all local events. Mouse, meanwhile, was known for being quiet and small. He squeaked in the morning, at the market and at all local events.

'One day, news spread among the animals that the other villages, who were jealous of the village of Ado, had conspired to steal the town's bounty. The village of Ado needed someone to alert the villagers quickly before it was too late.

'Mouse had been practising his squeak morning, noon and night. The villages were so used to Hen's cries that they ignored her, but Mouse could do it. He dug deep inside and let out a loud squeak that alerted all the villagers of what was to happen.

'The goat that bleats the loudest is not necessarily the most famished,' I finish, whispering the last line just like Mum used to.

'I thought the story was about Hen and Mouse. What's a goat got to do with it?' Teni asks.

It's the same question I always asked Mum.

I smile. 'What do you think it means?'

My question rolls around in Teni's head for a minute. 'Erm. Mouse surprised everyone by how loud he could squeak?'

'Yeah. Appearance isn't always the reality.'

Acknowledgements

Firstly, I wouldn't be here without God, so I have to start off by thanking him.

Thanks to Lauren Gardner for loving and believing in Sadé as much as I do and for keeping in touch while I was writing the book. Thanks to Justine Smith for picking up where she left off.

To Polly Lyall Grant, Sadé is as much your book as mine because we put blood, sweat and tears into it and I'm very proud. To Bec Gillies, Emily Thomas, Laura Pritchard, Joey Esdelle, Samuel Perrett and the rest of the Hachette team, thanks for all your hard work!

To Tope, thank you for being my forever champion. To Mum, thanks for always being inspiring and prayerful. To Dad, you once said that you'd publish one of my stories, but Hachette beat you to it. To Mark, we spoke about our futures years ago and now it's happening. I want to thank Tomi Oyemakinde for being my critique partner and my forever sounding board (you know your part in this book). To Debs, my sister and friend, for always being there through the madness of life. To Mariam Khan, my first writing person and cheerleader for life. To Louie Stowell, thanks for reading every and anything I send you. To the Fem 2.0 group: Amy McCaw, Louisa Danquah, Vanessa, V, Jamie-Lee Turner, Claire, and Kat Corr.

To my wonderful friends and family: Enitan Odeleye, Bimpe Eshilokun, Tola Okogwu, Yasmin Sahara, Dolapo Okunlola, Luellma Koranteng, Blessing Alade, Thara Popoola, Lydia and Daniel Riley-Poku and Abigail Alade.

Special thanks to Deborah Balogun for checking the Yoruba and for being an amazing friend in general. To Kemi Omijeh, thanks for checking all the counselling sessions and support group chats. Your feedback was so vital in making it authentic! To the Providence Hospice of Seattle's Safe Crossings Program, your support group resources were instrumental in helping me craft the sessions.

To Rumbi, I will forever be in love with the cover and the illustrations. You're so talented!

And to anyone else who I've forgotten, thank you!

Also available as an audiobook

Photo © Dujonna Gift

Rachel Faturoti is a writer, editor and poet with a passion for broadening the scope of authentic Black representation in YA and children's fiction. She believes it's important for readers to see themselves portrayed well in stories. Rachel's favourite books are *Skellig*, *Coraline* and *A Monster Calls*.